Queenie

Queenie

A NOVEL BY

Hortense Calisher

ARBOR HOUSE
New York

For Beecher and Barbara Moore

C O N T E N T S

ONE

Queenie: COMING AND GOING
Queenie: A HEART WITHOUT ENVY

Queenie:

❦ COMING AND GOING

A HAPPY childhood can't be cured. Mine'll hang around my neck like a rainbow, that's all, instead of a noose. In today's world, Miss Piranesi, who doesn't know which is more practical?

By my age—and whether or not the whole village of Fifty-Seventh-Street-and-penthouse-Seventh Avenue is drawn up at the gates waving Queenie on her way— doesn't any girl have to get out and start answering the lyric always going on between the legs? Day and night, what a musak, walking us down the street, waltzing us in a car! Safe to listen to only in bed, when it's loudest. Or dream-boating in a deck chair at ten past five. What's the difference I know who's singing it? Only the little man-doll, man-image, all virgins keep down there.

Sweet man-maidenhead, red robin-bobbin of a dollbaby, after doing all those drawings in anatomy, I'm still stuck

13

with you! Just like any ugly orphan of the storm, I still have to deal with you. And I'm going to have to do it in my own style.

I was born and raised to be a kept woman. Nowadays, women are no longer kept. World War Two put an end to it, long before I arrive. I get the bad news when I'm eight, and being dandled on my Uncle Oscar's knee. He's an honorary uncle, through my Aunt Aurine. The courts might call him putative.

"That war put the kibosh on it," old Billy Batong says. "High-steppers like your Aurine and my Vixen; they don't breed 'em like that anymore. The amateurs are in!" As a one-time owner of the Derby winner, Billy names all his horses for his past mistresses, except for the current mistress, who is named for that horse.

"Girls feel they have to be free to work now, even if they are pretty," my uncle says. I can hear him worrying about talk like this in front of me. Two years later, when I'm ten and chesty, he won't dandle me anymore.

"This new war!" Billy has three chins above his collar; all of them gobble. "Oscar—you realize men nowhere near our age, *young* men, are putting all their money in *wives?*"

In my aunt's arrangements, which include mine, I know well enough what that means. With a great bawl, I slide down off that knee and start running, out Oscar's huge mahogany front door into the marble hallway, and not

waiting for the elevator, up flight after flight of the old
joint, past more such doors and more marble, to the sky-
lighted top, then into our own wee door, out across the
terrace, and in again, through the French window of the
boudoir-bath where at this hour she can always be found
attending to her nakedness—(maybe toning and tinting
her nipples with the kid-covered nailbuffer whose loss always causes such a furore) meanwhile sitting in a paste of
rose water, pumice and almondmeal on her sponge-cov-
ered piano stool, slowly revolving for her bottom-skin's
sake. All the way upstairs, I hold the bawl in, so as to deliver it in full at her feet—which I do just as she looks up
from rougeing them. "Aurine! Aurine! Why do there have
to be wars!"

"Queenie's questions are always personal," Oscar says
later.

"And why not?" says Aurine. "A sense of proportion
is everything."

Every girl starts out in the same impossible situation,
right? Home! But how's a girl to leave home in the normal way, when the place is a love nest of illicit love love
love already?

Look at it now, blushing up at that helicopter in the
afterglow! In my real youth, before puberty, I used to
wave at them. Used to think they knew everything, those
penthouse butterflies. And every house on the route.

Queenie

Maybe they do; don't they work for the world's most experienced airline?

Yoo-hoo, Pan A-Am-m! Remember me? I'm the same kid used to spyglass you from down here—that rose-covered farmhouse-type penthouse job just two blocks across the air from the Central Park Sheep Meadow, where you used to land the President. Want to bring me somebody—I don't know who? Want to airlift me out of here, I don't know where? I'm a big chick now, ready to be an old man's plaything or a young man's darling. In three years, I'll even be voting. . . .

Bye-bye Pan Am, I Ching of the airlines. I may have to go to college, or dive off this roof into a country marriage, or wait my turn for an Onassis, all because you wouldn't look back. And inside me, I did wave. I'll wave at any astronaut who'll answer one routine question: Little love house, house of one's youth, how do I get out of here? Without just fucking my way out, like everybody else?

Out here on the terrace, the park is sending up all sorts of perfume feels and messages from the real central-heating-and-plumbing plant of the once and future universe. Rooftops always make me feel like a heroine, even though I grew up on one. Comes of being taken early in life to all those matinee plays with verandahs in them; Aurine's crowd swarmed to those.

From here, you can see at least five other penthouses,

though there weren't that many, once. Not on those two new high-risers on Central Park South, for one thing, where part of the tenants' kicks, they say, is having a view by blocking other people's—if you're an embezzler, you just naturally make for there. Our little sky-village, that maybe only I keep track of, gets a new bunch of cloud-tenants every time two investment realtors rub together. Six new forty-five-story towers are going up at this moment, between just behind the Plaza, to the northeast, and to the southwest just in front of the MONY tower, which has also lost that little Broadway church which used to crouch behind it like Old Dog Tray. But by flicking an eyelash, I can still see a four-block radius of old-time residents —I gave up the binoculars a long time back.

"Why, you people live in Central Park South's back yard!" a man once says to my aunt, meanwhile leaning over our parapet in that sporting way the garden-floor types do. "Or, are *they* in yours?" He's saying out loud what I often wondered. At going on sixteen, I was just then being fascinated to find out sometimes people do. I still am. What may I be saying out loud that other people only think?

"Eh?" he says, wheeling around to me with a great air of sudden notice, though at the time I am quite a tall pre-sixteen. He'd been pretty busy noticing my aunt of course; maybe that's why Oscar brings them, a constant stream of what she calls "Oscar's art guests"—men who appreciate beauty, and Aurine. She tends to dismiss them with the

plainest hint that she considers them unsafe, for whom
and what is made clear. Oscar and I watch these brush-offs
with pride; they're expected. She's our joint treasure. But
it all begins in her being Oscar's. And ends there. She
wants us both to know that. Him because to make a man
feel sole possessor is part of her professional training. And
me because, though she half-denies this, it is someday to
be part of mine.

"Eh, little lady?" says the man. He has a face like a mas-
tiff, and maybe's caught onto some of this. "Who's in who's
back yard? What do *you* think?"

Trouble is, I never can decide. Our building is on the
Mayor's landmark list; compared to us, the ones that face
north to the park, Essex and Hampshire House, the New
York Athletic Club, all that muck, are johnnies come very
late. The old joint was here first—and the old joint faces
south. So aren't all of them in our back yard?

But it's only by courtesy—and legal setback—that we
still see the park, not entire like we used to, only little
swatches of it. At first look, only the long, tree-pillowed
path up Central Park West to the Beresford. But then, if
you move way east on the terrace, suddenly all up Fifth
Avenue. The mysterious east, all the way to the Bronx!
By courtesy of the wild, jumbled surprises in a city's upper
air. Still, we're the ones who have to move to see it. So
aren't *we* behind *them?*

I'm so glad he sees the problem, I blurt more than I
mean to. "But that's one of *my* questions!"

Everybody laughs. But you always get something by letting a real feeling drop, even if you haven't intended it. I see Aurine hadn't known I had any she couldn't answer. And that Oscar already knows I have a lot.

Just then two of our neighbors, a couple who have a terrace halfway up that nameless building to the northwest about a block and a half away, come out on it. They grow things, you can tell the seasons by them, and that they're devoted. Things get much homier, over toward Eighth Avenue. Our guest sees me watching them. "We call them the Doves," I say. "John and Mary. Because they're a love pair. And because we never see them in the street."

"My God—suburbia!" says the man, I never got his name. Once in awhile, though Oscar himself doesn't see it, I've a feeling the men he brings aren't giving their real ones. "Ever speak to the ones you do see?"

"No, it wouldn't work out."

"Oh?" He gives me a sharper look, from that doggy face. "Who are some more?"

"Look down there." I point at an older terrace, low down across Fifty-Eighth. It's been screened-in lately, but there's still nothing on it but the feeder for the Dane. "She's blonde and tough, German we think, around forty-eight. Always wears beige. Whittled-down trousers and wraparound glasses, old ski-and-Garbo stuff." She's always on the street, buying a newspaper at the stand on Seventh —or in the park. Once I got near enough to read a charm bracelet, halfway up her collection, that said URSULA.

Which fits fine, but is enough. "Oscar and I call her The General's Girl Friend. She sometimes talks, but only to the fags with the really big dogs. We think the General's been dead a long time." And now her dog isn't a Dane anymore.

"Really. I gather they weren't a love pair." He squinted down over a passing pigeon. "What dya feed the livestock up here, Queenie? Cockail nuts?"

"Nothing." We discourage them. Building rules for one thing, though everybody knows the grocery downstairs stocks feed for a few old lady rebels' windowsills. And for me once. Who Aurine let keep the dirty one flew in my bedroom, as well as all the kittens and pups I might yearn for, never telling me how the pipi and shit went against her French ways. Oh it's been a happy childhood all right.

"Nothing? For shame. What kind of a village is this?" And he reaches over for a handful of Oscar's favorite pistachios and throws them over the side.

We all freeze. Strictest rule bar none, even climbing, from the time I was first let stay alone out here. Up here, a pebble becomes a missile. Straight across from us, in the newest high-riser over there, is the largest terrace yet— though a cheap crowd lived there then, junk piled back of their bedroom draperies. . . . Beginning terracers can be funny even when they're nice; they're like people who think private houses are private. . . . But like Oscar says, that kind are New York's scariest—corporation hipsters on a two-year stand and expense-account bread, next year the vice-presidency in Phoenix. The kid rode a two-wheeler round and round, and the week before he was dropping rocks on cars. We called the police, of course, though we didn't give our name. We're citizens.

"Sorry," the man says when he sees us. "Broke the house rule, did I? Guess I ought to be on my way. But what a dear house. That chimney, and the oval window. Duplex, too, isn't it?" He passes his eye over the black-and-white awnings from Normandy, torn now, and the espaliers that died, and the boxbushes due for burlap pretty soon now, that everyone advised Aurine no. "I never saw anything that reminded me more of Cornwall. Not even on Bleecker Street."

"Good-bye," Aurine says at once. It wasn't that she minded him. She was smiling, though I wasn't sure she saw the joke. It's just that she never urges any man to stay. Not even Oscar. Besides being very literal, as most all the beauties in our set are.

"'Bye, Mr. Selwyn," he says. Those who didn't know my uncle well enough to first name him always interested me; they were from outside. Oscar was running a lecture bureau just then, his usual sideline when he's brokest. This man could be the big-game hunter, or the ex-Commie ex-Catholic convert to Zen, or maybe the dolphin expert. He wasn't the pygmy or the Navaho, I could see that. " 'Bye Queenie. I like your village."

"Oh, don't go," I say. "You couldn't know the rules." I who never speak up in company, and am not much spoken to! Even if Aurine comes from Ninth Avenue, she is French.

And just then a pigeon shit on him. My aunt runs for a cloth. Oscar paws the air like always when he's upset; when we were asked for observed gestures in acting class, I gave it as his characteristic one, though I didn't explain it. He's smoothing his homburg, if anyone really wants to know.

"That bird thinks it's an eagle," says our art guest, wiping his head. We all laugh back at him, in trio, as we do at our best.

I remember it all—how we all stand there, helpfully, and in the pleasance of somebody and something tidied, at half past five of an evening just like now, daylight time not gone yet but not bikini season anymore, in the dark cool of a brilliant storm holding off, olive and orange in the west, to the northeast the whole misty moisty town, and between them the park that tells us our weather, our inland sea. We're a strange place if you could see us, Miss Piranesi, and I suppose a strange family, in our cottage set in the skyscraper mountains, me with a mother who is my aunt, and a father who's my uncle they say, and doesn't live with us, quite.

All loving and loved—why, that's nothing to be that, not in my aunt's métier! Which is so comfortably padded for a child to grow up in, in with all the other pretty ladies, Aurine's card crowd, and their by-blows. Not many ugly ducklings among us, we are all pre-selected, on the mother's side. Pains-in-the-ass some of those kids, of course, but still Saturday afternoon company, with all the women discussing our points above our heads and all our history known to them. All the way from the real lace on my confirmation pants (they know the very dress of Aurine's it has migrated from) to chuckles over what Tekla's son Giorgio and I had done in the bathroom or been prevented from. Right down to some hard talk about real importances—shall the mole near my left lip be let stay for a beauty mole? Only yesterday, Aurine reported slyly that Giorgio, whom we hadn't seen much of lately, had stayed out all night.

. . . Sometimes there were uncle troubles. Or business ones. Or well-known combinations of these. But then the presents erupted again, and what fancies they were—diamonds from Van Cleef, under whose weight a girl could scarcely lift a finger to trump her partner's ace, or those enamel-encrusted icons from La Vieille Russie, bought on Tekla's hint to Oscar, that lit up a whole corner of our sitting room. The girls all gave advice to each other's protectors, and helped form each other's taste—which by now, in their forties, is very high on the Parke Bernet department. And doesn't do badly on stocks . . .

But two years ago, back on this same rooftop, under almost the same sky, I don't think any of this, I only know, suddenly, my happiness and luck. I'm never dizzy up here, anymore than an antelope would be on Chamonix, but that day I feel dangerously able to fly. Or if I reach out

23

and catch a bird and throw it, all of which seems perfectly possible in the rose-yellow silence falling now on our four faces, it would come back to my hand to nestle there vocalizing, a cuckoo boomerang. The house itself, dimming and rising in the dusk, ready to soar off into the Hudson sunset with all its buttertub flowers like a bouquet for Jersey, is still solid under my feet—I know it's only my vision, my vertigo, that's performing here. It wasn't the man at my side—though I'll always remember him nicely. Or the twilight hush into which he tells us he's going abroad, and where—even that word stretches the beautiful horizons far.

. . . It's what is called a concatenation of events. Or, in my old Latin book, *natura naturans,* nature naturing. It was all of a parcel. That is, I am. The storm has passed over and I feel its salt like a whistle in my trembling teeth, and in my shaken ear a magical chord, "—Switz-er-land."

How can one all but faint away in the blessedness of all things come together in colors, in aunts, uncles, landscape and weather—and not have people pay the least attention to you?

When I come to, Aurine is giving him her hand, much more friendly, telling him her ancestors came from there, and he is kissing it. And Oscar doesn't look at me much.

Or, since I've grown breasts, tries not to. So there I am, hot and cold on my own two feet, with not a prayer of what has happened to me . . .

It's nothing really—as a British client of Oscar's once said on television, after the emcee asked him to describe how it felt to land the gondola of his transatlantic balloon when it began losing gas 14,000 feet up over the sea below. He was never asked on television again. But I hope to have my experience over and over, maybe in other company. For it was nothing really, except the beginning of everything. It was just that I'd never had an orgasm before . . .

So then of course, I feel so grateful and open—the famous female feeling, Miss Piranesi—and have to put my gratitude somewhere, and by instinct, or more likely training having its effect at last, turn to thank the nearest man for it—not beyond noting either that he wears a Piaget watch—and say to him what everybody does remember: "Oh—the best view's from my bedroom on the other side. Would you like to go upstairs and see it from there?"

"Alexandra Dauphine!"

But the mole at the corner of my aunt's lip—a beauty mark no one disputes—is lifting. Also, maybe she too has seen that the portfolio under our guest's arm is that costly, turd-colored calf which comes only from Hermès. But Oscar too is beaming, and he never knows things like that. I'm their darling, that's all—oh, happy noose! Why is the love you're sure of so much more troubling than the kind you're waiting for?

25

Queenie

The stranger is giving me the once-over, my first. Or the first I know about, from a man like that. Under that eye (all I can see now is that it was hazel) the skin on my left ribcage twitches—a little muscle I'll come to know well in the next four years. And the belly around my navel is blushing, reaching; like a kid, I look down to see. Finding only the brass buckle on my hip huggers, which I've cut off at the thighs, to show body jewelry pasted all over them. A juvenile mistake; good legs never make me feel amorous even when they're my own, and a girl should push only the parts of her body that do. Half the pushing is for yourself, isn't it?

This man doesn't look at my legs. Not to begin with. The truth of one of Aurine's countless adages hits me. "The best ones never do begin there."

. . . Dear Aunt, they all come true, your adages, your men. I've been watching. Why else must I leave you? I can scarcely bear to have you open your mouth these days; my future's in it.

That's why I wish I could lift my own eyes—in the violet glance you say any dark ones can acquire—and scrutinize that stranger again, giving him the eye from top to toe. In a way I can, turning out his pockets, zipping open that *objet* from Hermès, warming his watch in my palm, and breathing softly over the gray behind his ear—going all over him, like the expensive little kitten, scratchless for him, that I am being trained up to be.

But I can't see him himself, and I'll never know his face

or name. I don't need to. I'll know him, whenever I meet him, by all the other stuff I did see—and to hell with the brand of watch. He's not an important memory; he's a fact. He's around, all right.

He's the man Aurine and Oscar will be bringing me. Innocent dears, maybe they don't even know they were doing it that day.

He's the man who the world that bore you tries to bring you, no matter who you are.

What kind of household you start in doesn't matter; though Aurine and Oscar's way of life mightn't go down at St. Bartholomew's, a man like him is brought in there every other wedding day. He looks different in church, younger maybe. But settled, wherever he is, rich or poor. Our druggist's daughter married him yesterday—the druggist means his best for her. And she'll get it of course. Like me. Though I'd have a hard time explaining the similarity. Which way is more sinful let the druggist's wife and Aurine decide.

For of course the man I'm intended for isn't expected to last for life. He'll come by the half-dozen, maybe, all bearing a resemblance. I won't be asked to marry him. I'll be expected not to. But in every other respect, he's the same as in any village. He's the man the parents bring you, whoever you are. Or your aunt and uncle do, if you're me. He's the one who's enough like them.

So how can I tell them that even in memory, or present dreams, I never go to bed with him? . . .

27

Back there, maybe he saw that destiny. For he left, didn't he, on his own? Smarter than some others have been since. And with a bow to Aurine. "See why you call her Queenie."

Poor me, I'm still feeling grateful. So I follow him out to the little foyer we have, three marble steps down and a gold wicker basket to put mail in, and stand there, arms crossed over my bodyshirt, which is maybe the way he remembers me. "Thanks for the village," I said.

Aurine comes out after me; maybe she thinks we're making an assignation. She wouldn't mind that—"If it's time it's time, and you're *tall*" she'd say, she'd just want to know about it. But I was already alone, with what I'd never been alone with before. And haven't yet got a question for. Maybe it's nameless.

"Q'est-ce-que tu a?" she says, almost sadly. So I suppose she knows what I have the matter with me. "And where are you going?"

"Up to my room."

"I'll send up your supper?" This is standard. Tekla and her current man are coming to dinner, and like all her men before or since, he's a rough one for our crowd. They have him out of loyalty to her, and are always preparing to help her get rid of him. They have many kinds of dinners I don't share. Though I hear in Aurine's voice an uncertainty. Standards are changing.

But the little staircase to my room is just the same.

Up there, I go to the tiny window, an attic one between

28

lumpy dormers, much repaired, which hold you like clumsy arms. And in the pane's center is the brown campanile of Carnegie Hall. Yes, my village, and a fine one for any girl to come from, no matter where she's going to! Sur les toits de Meedtown Neuve York.

All the rest of the crowd, which means Aurine's women friends and their men, live over on the East Side, upper of course, in a number of typical residences—art deco, art nouveau or art bourgeois, Oscar says—whose probable incomes, passions and stability I could recognize before I could read. And like Aurine, the men don't really live with them. I always think of them as the real girls; those my age are just a sample lot for the production line.

Sometimes they do keep shops too, often only because the day is long. Which is responsible, my uncle says, for God knows how many misguided boutiques. Aurine wouldn't bother with that; she's a great business woman on a different scale, Oscar and I are sure of it, with many little nest eggs she won't let on about. We live on the West Side, and on Seventh and Fifty-Seventh, because as the daughter of the mistress of a certain restaurateur of the 1930s, what better way can Aurine show Fifty-Fourth Street and Ninth Avenue and that same restaurant, how far she's come? Only a few blocks away, she still has her village, which she goes to by choice on her own well-shod feet, never by cab. But in every other way, it is made to know.

Once a week, we dine at the restaurant *en famille,* and

once a month or more with all the beauties and their men. Long before Granny, who was Aurine's and my mother's mother, died, the place has a new management, but Oscar and I've begun to think Aurine has a piece of it. We see more than village respect for her life with Oscar, or even for the jewels she shows there and in the French Church at Christmas, in the way the staff says "Madame."

They say it even more so at the yearly party Madame gives them in her house, built on top of the old joint by a gambler of the twenties, whose aging girl sold it to Aurine. Thereby, Oscar says, keeping up the traditions of the original building, which belongs to the belle epoque.

And we sit on it, he adds, like the cream puff on the dowager. And on a lot of the tenants as well, for the newer they are, the more respectable. The rest of us are in the tradition; we might be anything and usually are.

Meanwhile, the weekly offers treble—to which Aurine says sweetly loud on the phone, "Our fun-nee ramshackle house, Mr. Mavrodopoulos, why it wouldn't be near enough good for you," then hisses over her shoulder, "They're trying to get together a package for an office tower, you can be sure of it!" Even when that time comes, she mayn't be on the selling side, for a reason I don't like to think about. And if I leave, won't have to. Girls like me don't get dowries; we are them. So call it professional backing for the pretty package that will be me. A family estate. Meanwhile all Aurine's satisfactions work out with hurt to nobody. And we adore her for it. Truly. I just don't want to be one of them.

Oscar's case is different. Though he was around Aurine before I was—from before my mother, her twin, died of me—there was of course a time in Aurine's youth when he wasn't around her exclusively and other men were; now and then he's made to remember it. Among the girls, this is called "keeping them up to the mark" and with either a weak protector or a strong one, I myself can see it has to be done. Their recipes for living the life of love have been dinned into my ears since forever; this is the basic one. And the main way it's done is the simplest. Oscar doesn't live here. You never really go to live with them. But if you are Aurine, you keep them a few flights down.

His flat's much larger than our house—nine rooms for a single man through thick and thin, and he's had a lot of thin lately. But Aurine won't hear of his changing; he doesn't know she's keeping up his dignity for him. When she goes in for doing that, she does it all the way.

"Never do like the wives do, Queenie, bolstering up a man for worldly purposes, and slapping him down for their own!"

She's been keeping up his dignity for years now. And hers as well. Not ever letting yourself fall in love with them, that's keeping *yourself* up to the mark. How much love is involved in this house is something I try not to think about! There's more than enough virtue around here as it is, to keep me from getting out.

31

At Oscar's, I've learned a lot of it. "Over at Oscar's," the most comforting words always. To be sent there on an errand when I was six, to run in to tell how I'd been kept at school, or still later to study in his huge library; it's been a second home. Which means the place that teaches you all your apples don't have to be in number one.

In the days when Oscar is a full-time impresario, the one that people think of along with Sol Hurok, a lot of personalities get used to Oscar Selwyn's little adopted girl running in and out, and I get to know them well enough to have to be careful to keep them out of conversation later; it's not standard, even at the High School for Deforming Arts, our rude name for it, to have sat on some of the famous knees I have. I sometimes felt Aurine sent me to Oscar's on purpose. In the confessions of courtesans, which bulk so large on her one-shelf boudoir library, these ladies, mostly too royal by that time to be called girls, often began their careers by being dandled on the knees of great men. Mostly, though not always, I sat at them.

"What's your school, dear?" asks a knee, and on reply murmurs to others in the circle, *"Ah yes, the last of the finishing schools classy enough for the déclassées."*

Later I confuse Aurine by asking if some project or possession is classy enough for us, privately resolving if so to have none of it.

Giorgio, who once went with me to one of Oscar's soirees, called it the School for Sotto Voce, and wouldn't go back. "They're refining your taste, Queenie. By insulting

what you are." It's easier for a girl to be a by-blow, even
without his classy one-side parentage. I learn a lot there.

Like having the greatest actor of his day purify my English, and a modern playwright quarrel with him over a
construction in it. For what I hoped was forever. Only to
see them join arms depressingly soon, to listen to a bull-
and-bears ringmaster from Wall Street, a few knees down.

I learn what Aurine and the girls never gave a moment's thought to, but women nowadays are so nervous
about—how men talk among themselves. It's what Mlle.
Maupin, if you remember, dressed in drag and set forth to
discover, though if she'd been me she'd not have needed
to. If most men talk to each other like the personalities
did, it's not what I'll set out to see the world for. "There
must be something more to men than what they talk
about," I report to Giorgio, who said, "Oh I dunno—
that's what we think about *you*." He's fourteen then, like
me, but precocious.

They talk about us of course, maybe that's it. At least
at Oscar's. There's some subtle thing about womantalk
that turns famous men commonplace.

Oscar says if my lot is to marry a commonplace one, I'm
to remember that.

He often slips and says "marry" these days, even in Aurine's hearing. And once he asked me, finding me reading
the Maupin, if I thought all men were swine, and I answered truthfully, "No, only Tekla's." After which the
separate dinners began.

33

Queenie

I know they worry over how to keep my viewpoint fresh, though they don't share the same viewpoint on what it should be. One thing they don't have to fret over: I'll never be a dyke. The day comes, even for a girl on the knee of the greatest name in Hollywood, when she knows she better get off.

Oscar's always been shyer with me than his friends have; after all none of them has legally adopted me. But although Aurine keeps her own maiden name, the restaurateur's Amidon, he always introduces me proudly enough, "My ward, Queenie Raphael." His real name. Selwyn is for theatrical. Or sometimes, depending on the man, "My ward, Alexandra Dauphine Raphael." Not bad, by my aunt's bookshelf. But I don't mind; I've got a lot of Oscar's bookshelves inside me by now, as well.

Giorgio admits he misses the library after he stopped going there; he says he couldn't use a man's house in the daytime if he wouldn't go to his parties at night; he was the most honest boy I ever knew. He said Oscar's was where we each came to terms with our possible paternities. Only, since he knew his all too well, while I sat reading all the romances, in the dark winter days after school, he read the facts.

Those winter afternoons, over by the time I went off to school, are like a piano under which we still lie, not touching anymore, building our separate trains, hunting

34

their terminals. Reading all the old novels and confessions I can find, and some accidental history, I see that lots of fathers have died before the kids were born. But not so many mothers have . . .

If I'm really Aurine's child by whomever, instead of being her niece, then she may be concealing my real age by several years, which is natural. On my own evidence, I've always felt older than I am, but then girls do.

On Gran's evidence, if I'm her other daughter's child, then by the date Gran seemed to think I was born, my mother was in her grave at the time . . .

Giorgio and I go up to Woodlawn once to check her headstone, all in order; she died two days after my birthday, not before. But a whole year before, if I can trust Granny's shaky reference. I can't. As Giorgio said, Gran was a wonderful old lady, but there was never any reason to *trust* her.

. . . Since Gran was away at the general time of my birth, taking care of her restaurateur's last years in Villefranche, she couldn't testify for certain which of her twin daughters I came out of. And at the end of her life—a little woman with pouchy cheeks, saying "It's where I keep my wisdom," sitting at our fireside like a nannie and with a nannie's name, Em Harrison—she mixes up the two like a pudding made of daughters. And nods like the nursegirl she'd been before the Frenchman took her out of his house to be his cashier—"Whose girl are you, what does it matter? Mine!" She's in Woodlawn too . . .

35

"What if I was twins, too, really," I say to Giorgio. "I mean, what if there were two babies, one for Alix and one for Aurine—and one of us died?" I divide the flowers I'd brought and put some on each grave; it's fascinating when life's like a confession about you. "Maybe the twins had you together, kind of a Siamese job," says Giorgio.

My own final belief is that I am my mother's daughter, but Aurine is jealous of it, and doesn't mind anybody thinking I'm hers. Especially since, though my mother was pretending to be married at the time, though not intensely, to a man I've no reason to suppose was my father, there's a rather strong chance, around the time I was seeding my way in from angel country, that I could have been Oscar's.

. . . Which could be true of Aurine also, if I want to go back to that angle; he was sleeping with both of them. Granny's viewpoint being, "It was all right for Alix, being kind of in wedlock, which is a mistake in the first place. But it was real naughty of Aurine to horn in on it . . ."

Therefore my aunt's jealousy: if I'm Oscar's, she'd rather I be thought hers.

I notice nobody ever blames Oscar. Once I carefully ask them, "We girls were discussing in biology—if a man is sleeping with twin women, can he always tell which?" Oscar chokes, and begins smoothing a few homburgs. But Aurine merely picks the top from a bunch of Malagas he's just brought, and sends me upstairs with it. "The twin can always tell," she said.

Let's face it, Miss Piranesi, we're a flighty lot, worse than the Polynesians, but I don't mind. We *are* a lot. A family unit. I never had to take it on love. They gave it to me. "If that's the way they want it," I say to Giorgio as the cemetery darkens, "I live with my uncle and aunt." It doesn't make leaving any easier.

But once I do, Miss P., won't I be in a position very like Gran at my age, when she left the nuns, over the same doorstep she'd once been found on? 'Twasn't religion that weighed on her, she said, or morals either; the world socked her with summat more serious. "'Twas that the guff I was brought up on, girl, wasn't most other people's guff."

. . . Oh Gran, even if that turns out to be true, you and the girls still gave me the best guff you had! I didn't hear about the mysteries of life, I got the recipes . . .

Like how the hair on that part of a woman should be brushed with an English hairbrush only. Housekeeping, that's what the profession is really! I learn what's "good" for my body just the way I learn lemon oil is good for mahogany. And what's good for me in a man's, in the warning that the way a man is formed—they never say "hung"—maybe isn't everything. And—how to thumb a man's eyeballs if he really means force.

Or like when Martyne, ex-Martha from Chattanooga, drops by for one of Aurine's mint juleps, I listen closely: Aurine always gives the recipe. "Jigger bourbon, crushed ice, mint, put the glasses in the fridge for an hour," this last slower, with the eyes closing. Then breathless, "Jigger of brandy at the last." Then she opens her eyes, says "It's the before and the after makes *every*thing," and I know she's talking about love—and that she once had somebody from Dixie. She never makes juleps in front of Oscar.

Bad language I never get from the girls; their tongues have a crook in them like a tea drinker's pinkie—they're ladies, not whores. Gran is franker. "Dirty language a man can get from his wife." And it's just as hard to learn the baby facts of life as in a normal household anywhere. Only the girls' temperaments, like their skins, are brighter, their ideas on it not so drear. Cabbage babies or Macy ones?—at six I know better; babies come from Argentina—"*Olé!*" or from Rio where Giorgio had, or when more workaday, at least from Aurine's dream-basement, where on a trip there she'd once bought six café filtres with silver suck-straws, and a bain Marie—the Galeries Lafayette. If anything, babies came in bain Maries.

There's no nonsense about wanting them, of course. But if we somehow get there, good grace to us—and a handmade layette. And adoration everlasting, from all the mothers in the set. Plus constant courting presents from the gentlemen, who continue but may not be the same.

"Oh Giorgio," I say as the cemetery gate closes behind us, "remember that bridge party at Nila's?" Where the only real ugly duckling among us kids, and the youngest, pops that pop question: "Where do I come from?"

. . . There's a full house that day, and each girl with her trademark. Hunks of Polish amber on the Slavs. Afternoon aquamarines on the Gabor types. A tiny French girl in three kinds of black. A Russian in riding habit and an Irish girl in Russian boots, one Andorran, one from Lichtenstein, and a Hungarian said to have the most beautiful backside in the New York area (two dimples). A pair of Spanish sisters like out of Lorca—how they ever separate is not known, and an Italian goiter-beauty named Alba, in a plain dress with a hundred seams, and a gold wedding band. And of course all the differing heads, billowing and coronet-braided, plus Tekla with her Swedish mannish and Riviera headband.

And the hostess herself, like a beautiful slim toucan, with a nose like little Ugly.

"Only he can't wear on his head what she does," Giorgio whispers to me—a frill of silk-petaled peonies and black water lilies balanced on an artfully streaming back-string. Maybe someday he will.

"Where do you come from, my plum—" she says to Nose Junior, in a voice like a warm accordion—a lot of them talk to us like that. "You came down a diamond drainpipe, darling! That's where you got that purple scratch on your heinie!" And maybe those pimples. But she grabs him to her breast, looking at the others. "Yes, you just squeaked through."

And four full tables of contract bridge look down at him, their eyes radiant . . .

In the subway from Woodlawn, I say to Giorgio, "I never have to wonder whether I was wanted or not. We

39

all knew I wasn't. At school, I wish you could see the hang-ups of some of those who were." Giorgio doesn't go to school; on insistence of his father's family, meaning dollars, he's tutored. "Well, I have to hand it to you," he says. "You don't look as if you just squeaked through."

Now . . . Giorgio. Not that I ever want you two attractive people to really meet, Miss Piranesi, outside my Platonic dialogues. He's out of the country now. But he's often on one of my mental clouds, overlooking me; you're still new to the job. On a lonely or a horny night, or a decisive one, this rooftop, as Granny would say, is fair damn populated.

Gran liked Giorgio, or thought he would do all right, which was the same thing to her. It's his mother, Tekla, she considered the idiot; in fact the whole set cherishes Tekla, as a good bad example for them.

"What chimps she always has!" says Aurine, after a fracas.

And it's true, Tekla's men may roar like lions, or look like hyenas, but in the end, they're always chimps.

Tekla is the type gets beaten up by bruisers. Who aren't always even bruisers; she brings it out in them.

In a house, I understand, the girl who takes care of customer demand for that sort of thing is called a donkey—though of course Tekla has never been in a house.

Her parents had a circus act in Stockholm—she ran

away because she didn't want to be the bottom of the pyra-
mid, even one made of girls. With her build she can take
punishment, and give. Not to Giorgio, though he's never
let her coddle.

Always in sandals—you can't throw a punch from heels
—Tekla's feet are like a scrubwoman's hands, red-knuck-
led and practical; the rest of her is like a six-foot Rhine
Maiden with a shiner just fading out or in.

Giorgio's built like her, only more of it, except for his
dark coloring and his feet, which are Papa's. Plus a certain
Latin narrowness to the face. He's something to see—in
the movies if he'd take offers; he says it would be bad for
his heredity.

His father was a famous playboy from the pampas who
married heiresses for a living; I suppose he couldn't whack
them. So practiced up on Tekla. And leaves her for the
usual reason: She started wiving him. Later when Giorgio's father dies of a bust appendix while bear-hunting in
Moldavia where his wife has taken him too far from penicillin, Tekla immediately has Giorgio's appendix removed
—he's been camp-counseling in the Canadian Rockies
since he was twelve "going on sixteen."

"Heredity," she says. "I'm against letting it work out."

Gran's still alive then. "Oh you don't have to worry,"
she says. "That boy's pure non-chimp."

Tekla has heard the word. "Giorgio's father was different!"

Since she usually only says this about the incoming ones,

41

not the outgoing or gone, I tell Giorgio this later.

"You and I always reassure one another when we can," he says. "Don't we? But she doesn't need to worry. I'm the boy without a navel."

. . . Every Christmas at the tree party, Tekla tells us that circus tale of the beautiful gymnast who appears in a circus come on hard times, doing tricks without price, until an angry rival tears his vest, revealing his secret, and the Christ Child disappears again.

We kids love it—"Tekla, tell us about the no belly-button boy"—afterward doing every handstand trick we know; what child hasn't wanted to be Jesus at least once? With or without his buttons. But I know for sure about Giorgio's.

"Sorry," I say, as we come out of the subway, "I've checked."

He's dark, but with a slow blond way of talking. Or did two years ago. How am I to know he's already thinking of South America?

"*Inside* us, maybe," he says. I can see he's hit on an idea amuses him, but also he trusts it. Visiting cemeteries makes anybody alive feel extra strong. "*Inside* us maybe, we have none."

We give each other the level look cradle acquaintances have to, then he punches me lightly in the chest with his rolled fist, says, "Oops, sorry, I forgot!" and I say, "Oh that's okay, I forget about them too." Which should explain our relationship . . .

He's the kind of best girl friend a totally male-oriented girl like me might be expected to have—a boy. Who isn't even a fag. On fags the girls in the set are openly puritanical; as Martyne says over one of her juleps, "Down home, lotta my boy cousins woulda been fags oney their mothers wouldn't let em. And I agree with that. Why should we women have rivals on both sides?" Rivals of any sort never occur to Aurine. Dykes irritate her some, the way costume jewelry does—both fakes. When one made a pass at her, on her first ocean voyage, the young Aurine kicked the lady with her first spike heels. "Between the legs. After all—a compliment."

But the real males, once the girls are assured of it, they allow every latitude; they love the smell of a dandy. Conceit can have as many vanities as they do, if it's a cocksman's. The more a man knows about female luxury, from sables to art, the better he buys it. "Why shouldn't a man sleep on silk sheets?" says Aurine, "——next to me!"

According to Freud, though, Giorgio should've been a fag—either on his mother's side or his father's. We discuss that the way we do everything, including what I ought to be; in each case this seems to have so little to do with what we are.

He says, "Guess my father dying so early for us set me free. So I can make what I want of him. Compared to the guys since, that's a cinch. . . . And Tekla, I'm fond of her, but I don't especially want to hustle her—I've tried thinking it, just to see. Nah, I don't even want to beat her. And the nice fags I know, I just feel sorry for what they can't look forward to. Compared to a cherry, what's creaming a guy, or buggering him? I think I just want to be good with women, in some of the ways that come naturally."

We've studied up on those.

"I like Aurine and the girls," I say. "But I think Oscar's soirees have the edge. I mean I don't think loving both of them's made me acey-deecey. I mean I sympathize with what the girls want, but I like the men for *being* it. When it isn't only dough, that is. I can't care about the bread. You suppose I want to be free to work?"

Giorgio doubts it.

"I want to be free for something, though. I can't think what."

He says that's one of the basic differences between men and women; we are compiling them. "A guy wears his balls close, his pecker on the right, goes for broke, and counts the dose later; a woman wears the rag on everything."

I know what he means (as events proved, he went after experience, in a businesslike way, and here am I, still mulling) but it's his language I envy most.

"It's a kind of Esperanto. My kind." He gets his source material from Tekla's current hunting ground, the UN. "Austroylian rozzers, Belgian *reel*politickers and Sinkapoor samurai," he says, his eyes sparkling. He cultivates it to destroy tutors with.

Miss P., have you ever heard "Waltzing Matilda" sung

44

in four-letter words ending with a Japanese obscenity? Or played an old spelling game called "Ghosts," using only what we call "body words"?—"I'm thinking of a six-letter word, female part, beginning with *s*."

We swap what we know for what we don't, trying not to let on which. Or we make up riddles, and synonyms: "When is a snatch not a slit? When it's a——" Maybe it wasn't always accurate, but it sure was rewarding to a girl who'd never heard the male part called anything but the "rector."

"The *what?*" he says. "Sounds like a thermometer."

When I dare quote my only new sources, the old wheezes I overhear in my waning knee-life——"Sam Newber says a wife is last year's mistress, with horns," he says: "Yeah, I saw his plays too, remember? All those actors in dinner jackets, tiptoeing like their dongs were full of soda water."

Sometimes I find a word in the fancy Victorian books he wouldn't bother with. "Gamaruche, huh?" he'd say, leaning over a passage. "Yeah, that's what it must mean. What a way to say suck you!"

Every sixteen-year-old is a pornographer, Miss Piranesi. We had to know what was open to us. But we weren't letches yet, or not for each other. "Not more than siblings are," he says. "Gee yes," I say, "incest sideways. What a drag!"

We aren't even dirtymouths, really. We're just trying to get out from under the old-fashioned background that links us away from other kids, and from the modern world.

45

We are just holding down our franchise to youth. Or I am. I'm still just uncrooking my tongue. He's all ready to uncrook his life.

Comes a time, though, a few months after Woodlawn and just before my rooftop adventure, when we're speaking only by phone; it's somehow embarrassing to meet. In-the-flesh has begun to have a meaning. When I ask him, last time we met, to describe a male orgasm—what I actually say is "pulling your pudding"—he says "Only a girl would want to talk about it."

I say, "Why, young massa, you sho nuf on yo way to beun a man!"

He softens. "Queenie, you need to talk to another girl." But he knows she won't have our frame of reference. "Too bad there's nobody in our crowd except the impossibles."

Our word for them! It's going to be lonely. "You mean you just want to talk to another boy—man."

And he says, in a voice I'll never forget, "I just don't want to talk anymore."

We don't need a manual on the basic differences any longer; we can just stand by and watch the action.

"Giorgio——" I can see by his face the deep water I'm in. I'm being a bore, and going on with it. When you feel *free* to be a bore, Aurine says, then it's over—you're a wife. And I haven't even been a mistress, yet. So I shrug myself out of that one, or try. "Well—we could always go back to the bathroom." We haven't done that, or anything, since we were nine.

"Uh-uh," he said. "Once a guy can't get it up with a girl he's washed up with her." I have to laugh. He has to. But I know I'm going to miss that frame of reference . . .

And how I do miss it, that night sur les toits de Meedtown Neuve York—looking out my cubbyhole, but still flying, flying in that beeline my body sends me on! I want to tell someone—that I've at least embarked. Not Oscar and Aurine, not because of who they are to me, or to the world, but for the same reason no young person ought to tell older people. They'd look at my secret life *professionally.*

My private movie, I think, leaning out to see the audience massing in front of Carnegie in the black-and-gold evening. Adults think of it *all* as show biz. That's what they say makes them adults. But could even a priest see much in what has happened to me? Like those saints who get raped while at prayer, it took even me by surprise . . . Besides, I always got absolved too quick for conversation. Most of the girls at school were miles ahead of me, and the boys with them; for them what I could tell them simply wasn't enough. Mr. Freud might've been mildly interested in my debut, but not for long . . . And for the same reason I can't expect the world to take me seriously. I'm not having trouble; I'm having fun . . .

Then, down in the house below, I hear Tekla arriving. With chimp. So—still unbloodied. Until the door opens on her, we never know. Earliest among my memories is Tekla and a chimp helping with canapés in the kitchen;

47

she says, "Close the cracker box, dear," and sallies out with the tray.

In our house, from woman to man, a traumatic statement. The admonitions must all come to us. Or seem to.

Behind her, Aurine says, "I give it six months." As usual, she's generously unaware the other girls haven't her talents. Gran barks out "One."

. . . And one it is—as well as the first time I see Giorgio leading in the bandaged Tekla, her both eyes blotto. With Oscar saying irritably, like to a client who can't handle himself, "Always the eyes, Tekla, that's dangerous! You ought to have lessons." And sometime later, "By God she did—she's learned *some*thing!"

Whereupon Aurine says no, it's just that the chimp has changed.

And Gran points out how Tekla never wives them exactly the same. "I've seen her carry that little rajah upstairs—for his heart. And make that baby prizefighter carry *her* up. So why shouldn't the way they knock her down them be different?"

The chimp then is a terrifying seven-foot-by-six-inch Swede they called "the bishop," because he dresses in what Tekla proudly calls "liturgical black." You can only hope the bones under it have meat on them. Strawberry hair pasted, unbreakable bifocal eyes, he's the kind Ingmar Bergman's camera creeps up on. Close-up: Hysteria. The strain of waiting's awful, for everybody except Tekla. I hear her sing out with, "We've had dinner invitations every night this week!"—she never sees why. The only thing the girls can do for her is to see she gets beat up in the company of friends . . .

Down below outside, the Carnegie crowd is going in; taking up my binoculars, among them I see a woman, one of the new tenants, who I once hear call Aurine "that outrageous person." Envy, Oscar said, of the popular ideal. "If I could find enough like that willing to book, Queenie, we three could spend the winter in Palm Beach."

But to Aurine it comes naturally. And to Tekla.

Oscar mistakes my expression, I'm not always sure of what it is myself. "Outrageousness is a quality like genius, Queenie. *Often* inherited."

He's reassuring me, this kind man who has the territorial rights in our house. Who I sometimes think is my father; who sometimes thinks he is. I don't look like him, but who could say for sure?—he's all loops; though he's a trifle thinner just now, his watch still hangs over his vest like a Dali. He's been the last to agree that the "moomies," as he calls them, are an art form. Which is why he's slipped, Giorgio says—an impresario has to believe in everything. "But I built my life on tangibility," Oscar says to Aurine, "I can't desert it now."

So she says nothing further, and pawns her diamonds for him at Kaskel's, which is just down the street. Also, charming one of the brokers there to let her slip them out on a party night, if needed. Whenever we're rich again, meaning solvent, she socks them in our own bank vault and

49

never wears them, sighing to me over this mystery herself.

"Will you wear them at Palm Beach?"

She widens her eyes at me. "Old women with face lifts, riding on tricycles—who would want to go there?"

Why deceive ourselves, Miss P., there's enough self-deception around to keep everybody happy, if we'll only give in.

But at nearly sixteen, I've already found out a part of my part of it. Leaning over my windowsill to see the last Carnegie-ite piped inside—what if like Hamlin, they never come out again?—I listen to my own music box down between me, still whanging out a tune from that other little tongue I've never yet dared touch. The truth about a girl's secret life isn't that she isn't a man. The truth is, she's not always sure of her expression inside.

Lucky the girl who hasn't a man at hand to tell that to. Not that I want to make it with anyone yet; I want a while to dwell on it. A time lag Giorgio says men don't suffer from. But we each have the same energetic background to deal with. We know we have to learn how to be outrageous in our own way.

Better to try it though, in a house without an extension telephone.

He comes on the wire quick enough at our signal: three rings, then hang up; repeat. Why bother? Because at sixteen you are still a pair of international spies reporting on what humanity has got you into, that's why. But usually he takes his time about calling me back.

When he speaks, it's kind of cautious, "Hello." That should have warned me; our usual game was to step right in and lead with the latest. Lucky or not, I always have a few saved up, not having his connections. This one is from school, via a bookshop on Forty-Second Street.

I say, "What's a dildo?"

He snaps it right back. "A false front." And then, in a molto snotty way he's never been before. "For a girl."

"Fags pad," I say, hurt. Up to now he's never pulled rank on me.

"You wanna watch these perversions, Queenie," says Giorgio.

I'm so slow getting it. "Know what Sam Newber says perversion is?" I giggle. "Afterthoughts." And when I told Aurine, she says poor Sam, maybe he doesn't know some men can think the same thing twice. But I never get to tell that to Giorgio.

"You wanna watch Sam Newber," he says. "Ever hear about that kid wanted to be a fag, only Mumma wouldn't let him?"

So then I get it, of course. Martyne would be the one. She claims only twenty-eight even now, and fourteen years since she came to New York with the retiring president of Texas Wesleyan; she's precocious. That's what men past their prime like her for. I put down the phone. I know what he wants me to say of course: We *heard* you stayed out last night. I can't. I feel like his mother. Women have this time lag. Tears even come to my eyes. We've been together so long, peering over the side, with our hard-ons. But he's into hard-core life.

"Are you there?" he says. "Queenie? I thought I heard a click."

If he could only have been on the roof with us all earlier that afternoon, I'm sure he'd've caught on to what's happened to me; I've already found that if I breathed deep, crossed my thighs and closed my eyes, I can all but repeat the sensation. But never quite. . . . I never can make it alone, Miss P. I'm just not queer for myself . . .

"I found out too," I said. "What I asked you last time what it felt like. Only, not alone." I only mean it kindly, in the interests of international knowledge . . . Double agents for the universe, that's what we females are, aren't we . . . ? "It's like—one of those underground explosions, isn't it?" And when he doesn't answer, I say, "At least it is, from the female side." I think I hear him breathing.

"Who's the guy?" Giorgio says.

"Oh——" He's going to be right out of our manual from then on, but I don't catch—it must take training so these explosions don't muddle the brain. "It was only halfway, really." How can I explain? "One of the art guests was around, and I—I never even got his name."

"Why you little c——" He shops short.

But I can fill it in.

How did we two end up screaming at each other; kids who'd been so close? Simple. Only virgins can talk to each other like we'd been. Experience shuts your trap. For that matter, only virgins talk. If we don't make out with each other from now on, it's going to be perversion all right. So we are only keening over the end of an innocent friendship. And the language we have for it is excellent.

"Fuck, fuck, fuck!" I yell. "What do I care how you say things—it's inhibiting!" He's insulted me. Without improving my taste. "What do I care if there's a hundred sixty ways to refer to a twat!" Knowing them wasn't going to change the construction of mine. Or Martyne's. "Mint juleps!" I say. "That—" I couldn't think of a single better word he didn't know of "—*dope.*"

"Well anyway, I'm not one of her cousins," says Giorgio.

In the silence I think I heard his heavy breathing; he must have thought it was me. Then he says, "We both went for it home-style, see Queenie? That's why we're so burned."

And that's why you leave home.

"How do you know how I go for it?" I say bitterly. How did I?

Right away we want to say it to them, don't we: if you had to screw somebody, why couldn't it've been me?

Maybe he hears it. "I'll rap with you, Queenie. A guy has to lose his cherry, he takes what's convenient, mightn't be his choice."

53

"If you could've screwed who you wanted——" I say, tremolo, "who would've you?"

"Ah—you know," he says, after a pause. A male rapping with you is a male already half out the door.

"Woo?" I say, softer than swansdown. "Tell me, woo?"

"Well you know, natch—who wouldn't? Is that you breathing?"

I make a sound like it is. I thought it was.

"Well natch, well okay——" he says. He's an honest boy, remember? "Aurine."

On which the phone itself opens up on us, like the house eunuch taking over. "TEKLA? YOU VISH TO KNOW VARE IS YOUR BYOOTY-BOY? OOPSTAIRS, VIT DER GIRL. TALKING FOOK."

It's the chimp, of course, on the phone downstairs. Then pounding up them.

The three of them follow after like a flight of aging angels to the rescue, of us two of course—they've seen Bergman movies too. Tekla arrives first, with the adrenalin of love, then Aurine, lightly, since she runs up and down four times a day for her hamstrings' sake. Then Oscar, puffing, but with a gesture my aunt and I are proud of; he's got the homburg in his grasp at last.

It's the chimp's head. In that position or not, its explanations make everybody furious. Seems he's a real bishop, not that Aurine cares, though she blackmarks Tekla plenty later for not knowing it. Seems he was only trying to phone his synod or something—"The Missouri Synod, Mrs. Selwyn."

Oscar says we are not from Missouri; she says she is not Mrs. Selwyn, both on the same breath.

All this time I've been letting the phone dangle in front of me, for my dignity's sake. Also to let Giorgio hear— kind of our last conversation. But now I hang up quick. Seems the chimp wants to *marry* Tekla.

She's not used to it. She beat him up.

Later I get four cards from Giorgio, who the next week ran off to Latin America, taking up his father's family's offer to be the princely heir; his father never married without a settlement. One card twice a year. The first one says, "I couldn't see myself in Rio still with my cherry, that's why." The next one says, "I'm letting my heredity work out for me. Down here, it's only money." The one after that says, "How you coming these days, Queenie?" I never answer. Not even the last one, which says, "Still think of you. See you in somebody's bathroom, sometime."

What can I answer, with a time lag like I've got? Sixteen, seventeen and still *asking*. One thing he and I don't need to ask; we've learned it together. Pornography, it's just recipes. That you never get to taste. Maybe I'll send him a friendly card though, when I leave here. Saying "Who can learn to be outrageous at home?"

But if you're a girl—and of a certain breeding, Miss P.—where do you go?

. . . Once it was simple, wasn't it? Poor girls, provincial

girls, perverted ones—Oscar says they all raise hell much the same way. But the poor can go into politics now. And where are the provinces? And if you're a nymphy—who's looking? And where are all the better men anyway? Not paying. So what bright girl would want to be an old-fashioned whore? On the street or in a house, or even on the telephone? It's a suburban thing now, for your afternoon kicks.

Also, my background for it is especially unfortunate. Aurine, Tekla, all of them, even Martyne—I could never face the girls . . .

So, in a few minutes, I'll get up, step through the French window over to where I hear Oscar and Aurine at their tea-murmuring, and ask a question or two. Foster or real, they keep up the pretense parents do—that they're my elders. Which means they'll try to answer anything. A child's role, as any kid knows, is to keep asking, for the impossible explanation; I've played it long enough. Not to deceive them, only not to trouble them. With what won't excite them like it does me. The plain fact is—I'm no longer that young.

I've caught on that asking can be a way of telling. "Where else better can I go," I'll say to Aurine, "to learn to be outrageous *individually?*" And to Oscar, "How can I bear to leave either of you?" Meaning—I've left.

. . . So, here it is, Miss P., all my background. When you're talking about yourself, don't you have to tell everything, especially when it will affect your whole life? Except of course in a love situation. But even there, it's better if women confide only to women. Where it doesn't really matter in the end, Aurine says, since all women on the subject of men say the same thing.

So, I'm making up a letter to be sent to a woman's college only. In fact only to you, Miss Piranesi. In fact your college is my first choice because of you.

". . . Just these forms," you said, handing me them. "And a personal letter." You couldn't have known the impression you made—nonsense, of course you do. A college that can have you for admissions head—in pants, false eyelashes and a Courrèges belt—must be something. You've made the best of yourself, and with the material you had to work with, that didn't take much doing.

"Personal?" I say. "How do you mean?"

"However *you* mean it," you say with a smile. Orthidonture, you've had it. From God, and from the Italians. "What you want to study, and why maybe. And of course, why you want to do it here."

Then you have to talk on the phone; those three rings on your left hand might mean anything. I think you're probably capable of anything, but will choose with care. That's my aim, Miss Piranesi, too.

"Short or long?" I say when you hang up. "The letter." You get up then, with a patient smile, and I see you really havn't seen me yet. You see so many. So my mettle is up; usually people see me when I want them to.

"In good or bad faith?" I say—a catchword of Oscar's.

57

That stops her. Maybe she notices my Dior scarf, I made it myself. "Lies or truth?" she says. I nod with my eyelids only, like her. I'm a quick study. She sees that. Is the ring she twiddles a wedding one, or only antique? . . . Anyway, you were interested, weren't you. "People generally lie," you said. . . .

But I'm not people, Miss P. I'm not even the younger generation, and I don't know anybody my age who thinks he is. Down to the kids just born, there's always somebody younger. Maybe *you're* it, Miss P.—about thirty-six, I'd say, looking ten years less. You'd do well in the profession, Miss P., maybe just a leetle more lemon juice on the elbows. And I know your name isn't Piranesi, just my joke. Any letter I'll send to the real name of course, with some high-class fudgeroo answers to "Describe your background, your aims, and what you expect to get from your study at this institution." You can hang it on the wall, to cool trustees with. But to you—this is personal:

Who I began as doesn't bother me—it's what am I going to be? What I am now, I already like; I can't help liking— some parts of a happy childhood you can't escape. But how do I make it from here? It's like what every girl wants to know about her rear, is it shaped like a *poire* or a *pomme;* I don't want to have to wait until I'm twenty-something, to look back and find out. *Somebody's got to tell me now.*

"Queenie has a question," Oscar always says.

Queenie has. Like: Do I have to go on protecting Oscar and Aurine from the way the world is now—or do I break in and tell them? Like: Shall I join the profession while I still can with a very big bang, being a virgin? Or just fuck my way around for the experience? Like: Don't you really get to know where you're going by going there?

I want to go to a college where I can get the answers to questions like this! And I'll pursue any course of study recommended. The world's got us girls coming and going, Miss P. Question is: Which ought to be first? Or can they ever be simultaneous? I know I'm old-fashioned; I was brought up to believe love isn't everything. And to use every wit I have, which frankly is considerable. But natch, that isn't intellect. On the admissions curve, where does that get me?

Please let me in, Miss Piranesi. I know rapping about what *I* want isn't the aim requested. But I've got one the college should be interested in; I don't want to drop out of things; I want to drop *up*. Far and wide. Meanwhile, here I am signaling. Letting me in will be letting me out. And of course I wanna meet men, the kind who don't know Oscar, and Aurine wouldn't want me to. I hear a lot of men go to college who can't pay. This is Queenie coming and going. This is me—in good and bad faith. Personally, I don't see any harm in not lying.

Oh happy, happy, happy! In the end, don't be surprised if I do everything.

59

Queenie:

❦ A HEART WITHOUT ENVY

WELL, I get there, Father. And thank you for your note. But does any other nice New York girl of today, wanting to go where I do, ever have such a thing with her folks over it?—like I'm a Gibson girl wanting out to a bordello, from the Newport château. Or have to go through the social occasions I have? Once my aunt and uncle decide to do anything, they do it in style.

First, a soiree at Uncle Oscar's, as not only the man who's kept my Aunt Aurine and me for the last twenty years in the style she's accustomed him to, but also as my legal guardian.

Then a staff party, in the ancestral Ninth Avenue restaurant that Aurine herself is a bastard daughter of, and that Oscar and I secretly think she still owns.

And finally, a blowout from all the crowd who've known me since my cradle, which is in fact the two-hundred-dollar lace-flounced bassinet they gave me. All Aurine's girl friends of her youth, plus the men who keep them.

But first I have to get Aurine and Oscar to agree to let me go. Oh, we all three know I'll go anyway, if I have to. But that is not the style of our house. Whose philosophy of love, and the love life, I've never yet quarreled with. And may never—I just have to find out for myself. We're a loving trio; our only differences began at my birth. For no matter who I was born to, sixteen years ago, Aurine and Oscar couldn't help already being respectively twenty-something and forty-something at the time.

So are they ahead of me or behind; who's in whose back-yard? None of us knows the answer. But we all go at it like soldiers—the business of working the two of them round so as they can pretend to see eye to eye with me. And, in the end, it's like they're only cutting the scarlet ribbons, smashing a bottle of Piper Heidsieck over my bows—no, there's a small château brand that's even better, said Os-car—and by the dawn's early light over Fifty-Seventh-and-penthouse-Seventh Avenue, putting me out to sea. Sea-worthy and beautiful as they can make me.

But like with any two unmarried persons who've reared their girl according to principle, it's maybe a toss-up whether college isn't the worst that can happen to me. Worse than a bordello, in one way. They're afraid of my getting married, of course.

That is, my aunt is passionately against all the things marriage doesn't do for a beautiful girl—to keep her beautiful, and a girl. Dear Oscar, like any uncle who just possibly may be the girl's father, is beginning to get pompous about it. Once upon a time, he gave my mother, Aurine's dead twin, a diamond so notable it's been left in a vault under my name through all our vicissitudes, and in the first flush years after, he also gave my aunt hunks of her own that she is free to hock at any time. Plus besides his friend Sam Newber says, "Years of morganatic devotion to a queen who won't make a king of him." But Aurine says Oscar's only like any smart man who knows the legalized evil in the hearts of men. And won't acknowledge what a smart woman can do about it.

He's beginning to think any daughter of his shouldn't be kept.

. . . I'm meanwhile remembering that time I was eight, hearing old Billy Batong, dead now, purchaser of that year's finest filly at the Saratoga auctions, mourning to Oscar that the era of great ladies of beauty is gone by. With each new horse, Billy used to acquire a new mistress. "War's ended women like that; men are putting their money into *wives*." And how I run wailing out to Oscar's apartment and upstairs to the penthouse he keeps my aunt and me in, bearing the dread news, with a question which has since become a family joke: "Oh Aurine, why do there have to be wars!" I remember every time since, that I've asked it. And each of her answers. Which are never quite to the point, yet are.

I remind myself how all my childhood, home from

62

school, unlike a lot of the kids there, I don't find only
the new maid and, "No, your maw went shopping maybe,
I don't know when," or just a note saying what's in the
icebox and the Democratic committee meeting will last
until seven. I find Aurine at her afternoon's boudoir at-
tentions to herself.

Before I was underfoot, maybe Oscar, and other men
before him, were meant to surprise her there. For she
never frightens us with blue clay masks and curlers, even
now. To me, back then, her rites already have a freakish
charm. Dear intent clown, she and I both know, with our
sidelong eyes, the solemnity of what I'm watching—a professional! What a man sees will be according to his lights,
however he sees this Venus—or Lola, or Marguerite de
Navarre, or Zsa Zsa—sitting on a milking stool, cooling
her behind in a bowl of rose water. She's never Marie
Antoinette; she's never dressed for it.

That day though, she's covered to the waist with a
peachy froth, scooped around her like the top of a Schrafft
soda, from which her nipples poke like the garter rosettes
she sometimes wore. "For a beauty mark, Queenie, but
never to hold anything up, the veins dislike it."

At eight, I too speak of all body parts with a "the" of
respect. I already know that love-in-bed indents the waists
"better than all those health wrestlers, the masseurs, like to
tell you"—and cheaper. And I know that never in her
life has she shaved her nape—from which her pinned hair
that day rears like a wave topped with its own comb.

63

"Never wear jewelry when naked, Queenie; it cheapens the bodyline." If you have hers.

At my yell that day, she drops her toe puff, stands up in her ruff of froth—white of egg, cologne and a dusting of cochineal, a receipt against sallowness—carefully towels dry her bottom, andante, andante, then takes up the English hairbrush a decent girl will always tend her muff with, and gives it one silky stroke. I am already soothed. I feel wars can wait.

Aurine has the luck to have a mouth whose ends turn up—or other women call it luck.

"Cozier than old Mona L. by far," says Oscar. "No man ever wants to draw a mustache on Aurine."

Her smile, if it is one, goes for comedy or tragedy equally. Whichever, when she proceeds to wrap herself first in the alcohol towel and then in her own invention, a huge one sewn entirely of silk powder puffs, it always seems to me the air lazily stops to watch. And when she emerges, her naked back to the window opening on New York's October air, a white cloud, tired and dirty as it must be from Fifty-Seventh Street, arranges itself nattily at her shoulder. I already understand that beauty is what this kind of thing happens to.

But Aurine's strength is you don't have to think about beauty with her; you can relax. "Aurine's a radical feminist," says Oscar. "She never stops thinking about men."

And in this dusky boudoir, no farther from a Marseillaise than I suppose boudoirs ever are, what potion are we

burning today, I am wondering—for them? And for ourselves of course, incidentally. In our house we're against
some things, including wives and marriages in my aunt's
case, and things like "the moo-mies" in Oscar's—his name
for what has been so hard on an impresario of the legit.

But against the male, in all his glory that we females
loudly give him? Never. How to be against him is what I
may someday have to go to college to learn. But at home?
Allons, enfants de la patrie! Men is what we're *for*.

So, I'm waiting. If my aunt answers my old question
about war in the funny Ninth Avenue French that her
father, old Achille the restaurateur, and my Gran, his
cashier girl out of a convent in Wavertree, Liverpool,
brought up the little Aurine their by-blow in—then the
answer will be serious. If she answers in her own English
—a hint of Granny Em's limey snark-and-barl, tempered
with Bergdorf-Goodman American—it will merely be
practical.

Stretching, she flings up and back a marble arm, à la
that bacchante statue with the grapes, used to be in the
Met. A favorite pose Oscar claims is based half on her
regrettable taste in art, and half on her respect for the
winter price of Malagas. Then she drops to her knees, all
naked flesh-art, rumples my hair to a better curl—"No
braids for her, Oscar; she's to be pretty from the start"—
touches my button nose, in the face she has decreed somehow will someday be hers, pulls up my panties, and so having thoroughly shaken up destiny to let it know what it's

to do for me, she stands up to the cosmetic bar where her bookshelf is of courtesans of yore. With one long thumb smoothing the memoirs of the de Lenclos, who lasted past seventy, she answers me—girl to girl.

"Billy been on that, again, has he?" Her thumb continues its caress of old de Lenclos; is she smiling? Or sad? "Billy's 'ad to give up steeplechase, poor old lad. Poor lad, 'e's seventy."

While I'm thinking what steeplechase is, comes her second answer. *"Pauvre* Billee." Her contralto moves us both. A finger crosses my mouth. "Shhhhh," she says. *"C'est la guerre."*

Some years later, maybe when I'm twelve, I overhear Oscar say of her to a friend—meanwhile not seeing me doing my homework in the alcove in *his* library, which is more extensive, "Aurine has a heart without envy. Penis envy."

Well, that's fine for her, I think, peering out at the two gents who've planted that barb and then settled themselves like clubmen, with a couple of gazettes from Oscar's table of them. Sneaking out the back way, I decide it can't be because Aurine's being saintly about it; she's just never that psychiatric. Then why does she have a heart without penis envy? Must be because she's seen such a lot of them . . .

As yet, I still haven't had her opportunities. What hers as

66

a child were, she's never said. But since she was a by-blow, just like me, and in a much more formal era, I imagine she grew up much the same. I can't think the old French-man went around in his BVDs when he came to call on her mother. And like Oscar, he didn't live in the house.

As for Oscar, he's been like a father to me in most ways. But in the exhibitionist department advised nowadays for girls' daddies?—nothing doing. He'd no more have walked around in front of babygirl Queenie with his prick showing, than he'd put it on display at the Modern. I've never even seen him without a vest.

Not that there can be anything wrong, Father. Aurine would never stand for it.

As for me now, has anybody stopped to consider that in spite of bathroom play at age five, the Museum of Primi-tive Art at nine, the backseats of cars at ten, and from then on any number of lively arenas and propositions, a girl rarely gets to examine what she's supposed to envy, in the calm and neutral light of day? Or of night. A girl rarely ever gets to see the male organ in a stable situation. Even in daylight, she has to take it more or less on in-stallment. And the minute she does, I suppose it tends to disappear again. Pay now—see more later.

What I think is: What a woman like Aurine doesn't want for herself, I can probably get along without. I'm interested in them like mad in a way, of course, but do I really want one for my own?

But then again, I argue, nobody else's experience is

yours either. And Aurine never knew Freud. *Can* a woman be happy and successful these days, without penis envy? . . . Chalk up one more reason for going to the brain factory. I have to wait till college to find out.

So every day for two weeks now, I'm hanging on the admissions letter, each day it doesn't come, lying here in a deck chair, talking over my anxieties with the clouds. They must know the national girl situation as well as I do. Just being pretty isn't a score these days. To be in you have to be intellectual; even a model getting interviewed for Hollywood tells you what she reads isn't just *Women's Wear Daily*. It's Sartre—on Sundays.

But it isn't only fashion that sends us to college these days, Father. Or even parents, though few are as against it as my guardians. And we sure don't go there to get married. If Aurine, and even Oscar in a way, can fear this, it just shows how old-fashioned they are. We go, Father, because all over America girls have questions like mine. We're the generation after the pill generation; now we want the directions that come with it. Something better than the "Go, go, go, straight ahead," that they had. What's straight? Where's ahead?

At least in the old days, when people said "Don't!"— you knew what to *do*.

And now at last I have the college's acceptance letter in my cool, unmanicured little mit. Sometimes, Aurine takes

my fist in her own filbert fingers and looks at it. She told
the Lord I had to look like her, and he bowed to that;
she must have an excellent relationship with the Lord.
Nothing to do with praying; something that gives her confidence. Whatever it is, she got it without getting a BA
for it. But I can see my hand puzzles her. After all the
trouble she took for me—with that hair, those eyes, et
cetera, and above all, that waist—aren't I going to do
more with it? The only thing we seem to agree about is
our napes.

Dear Auntie, how can I tell her the very real rough
nature of the competition nowadays? How can I tell that
beautiful pan, still without a wrinkle of its wisdom on it,
that all the girls I know, laid or half-laid, are pushing into
the think tanks with the same united question, *What are
we competing* FOR? And if it's a penis, Auntie, why don't
you envy it?

So, it's time to step inside that terrace window Aurine
had cut in the brick so many years ago "to catch the pink-
est light with." And tell the two of them the letter we're
all waiting for is here.

Every afternoon they're in the salon anyway, at their tea
—which is champagne for Aurine, and for Oscar, Carpano
—sitting under the remnant of the ikons which in the old
days Oscar now and then bought for her at La Vieille Russie. A good investment, she always said, that a burglar

wouldn't know about. Not so easy to pawn, as it turned out, and too easy to sell. Which is in one way or another the explanation for the absence or presence of any of our goods. In the current state of our finances, if I leave home for a dorm, something else will have to disappear. That's why they've been sitting there extra late these past two weeks. They're waiting for the college to tell me. What life has in store for them.

Letter in hand, I move nearer, around a cornice from which I can see them, a beautiful florid couple sipping almost in still life, in the slanting, interior flush of sun we get up here. Or that they bring to it.

My aunt is sitting under the ikon she loves best, of all those she's managed to keep. I see now she's saved all the St. Georges; how come I never noticed that before? Next to her, on top of Gran's old telly, is a fifty-dollar bill always left there for burglars, as an inducement to take both and run. Other people we know leave twenties, but Aurine's private style is the same as her public one—Oscar says that's what the grand style is.

He should know. His huge outline still has the nobility of the young baritone-bass who once—in Venice, at a festival, in the off-season—subbed a Baron Ochs at the opera house. His ties are still from Sulka, since Oscar Selwyn, worldwide impresario, splurged on more of them than lucky O. Selwyn, who runs a lecture bureau in a hole in Carnegie, will ever need. He is, he says, an amateur in a world he never made—and wouldn't think of making.

Even in love he refuses to turn professional. My aunt's cool, shepherdess shoulders, always bared for his visit, slide in and out of their curved draperies with her breath; any moment the chiffon will slip past the nipples' edge; the eye can't help measuring the possible fall, just as people do with steeplejacks. Familiar as he is with the forms underneath, he can't help watching. And though he knows their perfect anchorage. When he leaves, he will kiss her hand, his hat in the other. And twenty years of this happiness have not spoiled his face.

Above them, it's past six by the Venus with the clock in her belly that Aurine won't get rid of and Oscar surely didn't give her; by now he should be downstairs in his own big flat, at those serene bathroom duties which I imagine but have never seen. Afternoons are for his cronies down there, or for what's left of his business. Mornings are my aunt's time up here for our household or other projects outside—does she secretly visit him then? Sunday mornings he spends here, but far back as I know, he has never spent the night.

When do they do it? puzzled my childhood much like anybody else's. Now that I'm grown, my aunt's rhythms of love have long since been evident; she has a kind of overall blush afterward, pink as the stucco I'm leaning on. But since it can hang on for hours, or start up suddenly, right while you're watching her, in "a limpid laugh and a liquid eye," to quote Sam Newber—I still can't tell just where or when. She has to show her satisfaction of course, unlike a wife, who's not paid for it. That's what's wrong with wives, says Aurine.

. . . "How'm I ever going to do it on my own," I've often wanted to ask her. "With all *your* philosophy weighing down *my* organs?" . . . But now, letter in hand, I've no more hostility—I've never had much. I just want to ask the old riddles, get the old answers, and run like crazy out of here. How else can I manage what every loving young person wants to do for their older loved ones? How else can I keep them innocent?

So at last, I poke my head in, hand behind my back, and ask: "Aunt Aurine, why do there have to be wars?"

After all, a live question, no matter who asks it. Or who answers. The game is, in ten years of joking, she's never come up with the same one.

On the double I get it.

"Countries get angry!" Aurine says. She doesn't look at me. Oscar's quick glance doesn't have to tell me. She's a country—and she's angry. She's having one of her English days, when Oscar says she reminds him of the Queen on the telly, reviewing her regiment. . . . While the audience thinks to itself, maybe, of all the things that great Scotch tartan of a girl has never seen . . . except Prince Philip, of course. Does *she* envy *him?* . . .

Now my aunt raises her head, and looks at me. Above her, the ikons flame. "Something useful and proper always goes off after a war, Queenie. World War One killed off hats." Gran's last lover, a manufacturer of fedoras, bequeathed us this wisdom, plus one other—never trust a man in a borsalino.

And I'm going off. Like a hat.

"Didn't kill mine," says Oscar.

Then we three are silent. Wars are what they are, but a family joke has just died.

"Why do you wear that old coral?" she says, with the first motherly petulance ever shown me. "It dates you!"

Oscar gave me it at my birth—a Georgian coral. Which is a baby's silver teething rattle, knobbed and belled and big as a fist, with an inch-long red prong. I wear it on a chain and tell the kids it's a phallus. Certainly it's valuable.

"No harm done, Aurine," says Oscar. "Since it's George the Third . . . Queenie—what's it you've got there, behind your back? A yes? Or a no?"

I don't have to say.

"All that reading!" says my aunt. "You'll ruin your chin line!"

Oscar winks at me. "Long as it's not her eyes."

Oh, I know the ruin she wants for me—and in what style! Just as I know the worry they have for me. Like the Vatican must have for its new-style nuns: Whatever's in their pure hearts, their legs are showing.

And I can't help to conceal from these two loving experts what my free tongue has hid from my classmates. That though technically of course I'm not untouched by human hands, whole regions of me remain unexplored.

73

There's a dull word for that sort of female. It will never pass our lips. Not in this house.

"College couples seem to marry each other so indiscriminately," Oscar says. "Out of nostalgia, do you think, because they can't stay on? Don't just marry somebody, Queenie, so's you can revisit your sophomore year in the evenings."

"*Everybody* going to college looks rich and healthy," says Aurine. "So how will you tell which?"

All a parent really wants is reassurance. On what your temperament is. They just wanna be sure it's theirs. They can't wait to know. And they can't believe *you* don't know.

So I do what I can for them.

"Uncle——" I say. "I promise *not* to couple indiscriminately. Marry, I mean." I see that his new image of himself—as a pater—isn't quite happy with this. "Or—I won't let anybody set me up, unless he has your permission."

"Child, child, child," says Aurine. Almost a groan. A wrinkle has actually appeared between her brows. "Do you know your own worth!" That's the French side of her —she hates waste. But most of all, she wants me to *get on with it.*

What can I promise her? I think of what Gran said, how in her day the sheets still were examined for the maidenhead. Not in the Middle Ages either, Ducky—in Liverpool. "Don't worry, Aunt," I say, soothing. I reach out and smooth away that wrinkle. "Soon's I'm fucked, I'll phone home."

74

So—ten minutes of apologies. If we don't say "virgin" much in this house, we don't say fuck either. Sorry. It slipped out. But how did it come to be there, to slip? Do girls of today always go around thinking like that? No pretense—she doesn't. I recall Oscar explaining once why the confessions of courtesans are so mincing. "Ladies to the end. Even that end." But he doesn't wink now.

"Not always," I mutter. So the peculiar freedoms of our house, which I know as well as they, are restated. Finesse is all.

Except for money. Now I'm to go, they simply will not accept my plan to pay for it.

"NO!" Oscar says, with a great rise of the watchchain. "That diamond in the vault belongs to you!"

"We-ell——" How do I say it to them? "So do *I*."

"NO!" says Aurine. "I'll hock *me*." Meaning, her diamonds. . . . One way or the other, our personalities are a good deal involved with jewelry.

Later, Oscar tells me mine's worth too much to be any easy hock; the market would rather buy.

And Aurine remembers hers are already in pawn.

But right now, she says plaintively, *"Mesdames. Et Monsieurs."* And stops, looking at us oddly. Why does her own generous action embarrass a person? Answer, from Oscar later—because if it concerns money, money's not a good mixer, money's as cold and neutral as the universe. Which must be why he can't make it any more; money doesn't like to be ignored.

75

He's looking back at her. *"Oui, Madame?"* I realize I've never heard him talk French to her before. And what a lot there is between them that I, darling of their house corners, may never know.

She's quite unable to speak yet. I see a pulse at her temple. A beautiful woman, doing a gracious act that's difficult for her; shouldn't this encourage the stars that once in a while humans are worth holding the universe together for? Don't count on it. But closer relatives are much moved.

"No," says Aurine, in the smallest voice I've ever heard from her. "I'll get it. I can get quite a lot of money there. . . . The restaurant."

So! She does have a piece of it then. Bought back somehow from whoever the old man, whose bastard she was, sold it to? Certainly Gran didn't inherit the place; she could never have kept it from us.

Oh, if there were a man at the head of it now, Oscar and I could understand well enough how this violet-draped woman, with her bronze hair and non-smile, could get anything from him. But there's nobody there except the old headwaiter Marcel, and the owner is thought to be a syndicate. She must have a share.

"Cherie, cherie——" Oscar says quick. It means no, don't do it; no, don't tell me—probably a lot of things, including, "My dear girl, Queenie and I were always on to you, as you very well know."

Oscar's very complicated, but he seldom bothers to be

quick. Last year, a young man said to him, "These new Edwardian clothes become you." And Oscar replied, "Got them in Paris, at a price; you'll find the mannerisms come with them, for free." But he was too kind to say that this was all back in 1935.

"Ahhhh . . . *Cheri!*" Aurine says in a long, graduated voice, as if she's stabbing herself just below her pearls. Which are not in hock. She too is much moved. It's like Camille, like Réjane, like the divine Sarah—before her leg went; it's like Aurine's whole bookshelf. But since it's like her too, it's real.

"Oh she's worth it, our girl, isn't she, *mon vieux?*" she says. The pearls swell to an arc for him. The smile, from the heart of another girl, whatever's in it, is for me. But the voice that issues from it, sideways, is pure bourse. "Don't worry, *copain*. I won't have to *sell*."

She is the syndicate.

We both know exactly what it costs her to tell. Not just the natural fear of all the girls in her set of beautiful women from twenty to sixty, beautifully kept by men of all ages. A fear which at times takes forms much stranger than stocks or emeralds, or even ace-in-the-hole secondary affairs. Like with Martyne, who's now spending her take as a part-time bookie, on jockey lessons. And Alba, who every Friday leaves her townhouse and Maserati to go by subway to a law office—"Law stenos get very high pay." Or Dulcie, who does "something awfully tiring, Duck," for the government.

77

Aurine's courting a deeper danger. That Oscar will catch on that her private thrift, private fear, is for *him*.

In the world of finance, he must appear to be king.

Hasn't she often and often told me why? "Our world is cleaner, Queenie. We never make a man pay. Except in money."

Though she knows living cheap wouldn't bother Oscar for himself, only for her. And that's it, you see. At the bottom of this holding company of interlocking ownership. She can't let on to herself that she might be doing it for love. She has to keep *herself* up to the mark.

"I bought the place years ago, when it got rundown," she says to him in her softest voice. "For a song." That may be true, considering all sides of her. "Out of the housekeeping money." Then she rallies, in order not to think less of herself. "After all, in all New York——" which means the people we know in it, "what woman's had a higher housekeeping than me?"

Oscar answers smiling. "It can never be enough."

Next day, he sends her a bibelot, not from Alexander's, tucked inside the weekly orchid. Where does he get *his* secret income from, I wonder—at stud? Which since I've shocked them once too often, I don't say. For a whole week after, he has that queer smile on his face, for how well he knows her. And another not too different one, for me.

"In that bordello you're going to, Queenie," he says, "see that you do as well."

So it's settled, Father. And that's how I get out of the château.

It's one hell of an exhaustion, being an old-fashioned girl.

But it's not until the parties that I learn what's in my own heart.

Looking back now at the loving crazy quilt of coming-out parties they patch up for me: A Stag at Oscar's, with me the only doe; a Family Fuss at the restaurant, with no family but us; and an all-time Bye-Bye Blowout with the "girls" I can see from an aerial perspective of two months, which is plenty at my age, that they still think, "Wouldn't sending her off with a man be the safest?" And are still hoping God will intervene.

It's hard not believing in God, in my family. Harder even, Oscar says, than for lapsed Catholics. Aurine says, "It's because God believes in *us*." That's her theology.

And I believe in her.

The Stag at Oscar's

Oscar's soiree is my first send-off, Father. Too bad you were in retreat. It's only his cronies, dropping in more formally than usual, to what one of them once called the New York Athletic Club's Theater Wing. Some still do come in straight from the steambaths over there. All are of an age to benefit from them. And they've known Oscar's little ward Queenie all her life. They're my other uncles. Still, sixty men and a girl, and not one of them too young to be a father-image—how could God help getting a little interested?

Like in my childhood, the party is stag. And since it's for me, they all find this charming. The only change is from afternoon to evening. Plus that back then it wasn't me, in my scrawny leotards, whose points the conversation was appreciating. And now has just toasted in champagne.

"I feel nostalgic already," I say to Sam Newber. "I don't know yet for what or who."

"That's what nostalgia is, you nit. And you don't have to go to college to learn why." Sam's a sandy, marionette sort of person, polished very high, like one of his comedy successes of the forties I saw revived once. Very tuxedo stuff, with a few spiritual zonks for the male and female leads to sink into the sofa with, at the end.

"Maybe that's what *champagne* is," I giggle. I've always been able to talk to Sam almost like to a girl. Aurine can too —she says don't let's wonder why. Does Sam? "Imagine me not being able to drop in here every day, even for a coke."

Imagine an arched double living room, fifty by thirty, and fifteen feet high, darkish except for the yellow Tiffany light at the tops of the oblong windows, and everything furnished from old stage sets—only the solid kind of three-acters, that used to have drawing rooms in Mayfair or

80

Murray Hill. No flashy stuff, nothing surreal. One bent-
wood rocker, from Weegie Jones' farmhouse-ballad read-
ings of the thirties, that even then was a flop. "Oscar's
letting him revive it," I say. "But it still flops."

"A lot of flops are here," Sam says. "Some of mine."

A lot of very elegant ones certainly are, from yards-long
English breakfronts to those French bureaus that swell
out like women. And seventeen pair of portieres, Father.
Oscar says half of Paris comes into a room with that word.
The other half comes from the thrift shops on Third Avenue. Plus twenty club chairs in black leather, said to come
from the Hotel Marguery, which make it comfortable. I
sink into one of them. It's a room for men all right. Nothing cozy-chintzy. Or penthousey. That's left to us, upstairs.
This is the downstairs of life.

Two kinds of men are here. Mainly, Oscar's clients from
the big days, from the really famous opera singers, politi-
cians, explorers, playwrights and legit stars, down to diplo-
mats, royalties, tennis stars, any lecture name who could
have filled a hall, once. The rest are the stooges; nice little
guys who once worked those worlds in some way, colum-
nists and ticket brokers and press agents, and one very old
guy said to be the Barrymores' butler—I've never known
whether for stage or for real. As a child, I had no prefer-
ence; in one respect, all their knees felt the same. I knew
I was being dandled by men who liked women.

"It's been a great background," I say to Sam. I'm saying
it silently to all of them, who though they're deep in club-

men's smoke at the moment, won't have forgotten me and mine. These fine world-worn men, pledging their troth to me in cigar rings, and an occasional pinch, believed in us. And in spite of the scarcity of Cuban cigars, and the decline of the pinch—I believe in them.

Sam's at the bookshelves. "Oscar must have over fifteen thousand books here. And over a thousand of them must be real."

The rest are very fine vellum the stage designers used to buy by the yard. And set in a row of lighted niches under the brow of the books are the women Sam is looking at, in photos any size from one foot to life.

"Very selective," says Sam. "Oscar's not one to take everything he's given, is he?" All the girls in Aurine's set are there, each in the clothes of her big era—all the live ones. Sam is going down the line. "Why, I didn't know Lalla was dead," says Sam.

"Yes, Oscar never puts up a nude one until she's gone." When it's respectful. For these are the girls these men in their time have belonged to. Pardon—have kept. Now and then in rotation. Though it's true, Oscar doesn't take just anything he's given. Except for me.

I giggle again. "Once I asked Oscar who decided the size of the photos. He said, 'Modesty, dear.' "

"True," Sam says. "Here's Dulcy, whom we all love in spite of her CIA connections. Only one foot and a half. Always so self-deprecating."

"And there's Taffy Rhys-Williams," I point. "Who went

off with Tekla's rajah." No loss. But no excuse either. "She sent herself back in a crate." Five and a half feet of skin and pearls, and skin; when Oscar brought it upstairs to show Aurine, she said, "Well—practically dead."

Aurine never comes down here. Her picture's set a little apart from the rest, and is an oil painting, as a sign she belongs to the house. It's from ten years ago. In a dress you could die for.

Sam's staring at her. "Well, if you ever hang here, Queenie, you'll know who you—were."

I get straight up from the chair. "The girls are still stunning, all of them." Most. The ones who are not, are no longer one of the girls.

" 'Fear of fa-ding——' Sam's humming a song from his play, 'keeps us from fa-ding, dear.' Oh, they do very well. Your aunt of course is unique."

"Most of them are lots younger than——" I flip out a hand. Handsome men, distinguished is more the word, but attractive enough you could still die for them, I suppose. If you're in the right dress. "Lots younger than any of you."

"Sadly true, Queenie love. Here, give me that glass." He takes it. "But outside this . . . club . . . the girls are even younger than that."

"Not for Oscar."

"Oscar too is unique. Why, looky here." He's filling my glass from under the rows of pictures, where the bar is always stocked with the wine and seltzer, the whiskey and the beer. And tonight, the champagne. And the cigars. Sam takes one. "Cigarettes, you bring yourself. And no women. Oscar's an easy host. Easy on us." He lights up. "Nowadays, the orgy is only one of sentiment."

What's he trying to tell me, talking as usual like one of his plays?

"Ladies used to appear, at his evening suppers," I say. Catered from the Stage Delly, consommé to nuts. "Oscar's poorer these days." But I'm suddenly remembering how it used to be when I sat on laps as well as knees here. Way back. And way, w-ay livelier.

Sam shakes his head. "Uh-uh, that's vintage you're drinking. Oscar never stints anybody except himself. No —the word went round—years ago."

"No girls from the outside?"

He nods. We both look at the gentlemen chatterers, their familiar heads all down the length of the room, like those cartoons with numbers that tell you who. And beside each head, the invisible one of a girl who isn't here? Because if she were, she'd be years younger than Aurine?

"I don't believe it," I say. Sam's his kind of playwright; Sam likes things neat. Besides—Oscar would never do anything so vulgar. As pass the word around that Aurine couldn't take it. But most of all—Aurine's deeper than that. Or simpler. She could handle it. She'd love to.

"I don't blame you," Sam says. "No girls at *all*, you nit. Except you, you lucky creature. How many ten-year-olds have had a salon like us?"

84

I am too stunned to speak of course, for the moment. Because of me? They stinted themselves of social pleasures that weren't yet right for me? Oscar *and* Aurine. Why have I never thought of their doing something together? For love—they did it for love. Because of me, they haven't kept *themselves* up to the mark.

Can I believe it? Answer—once you're in the play yourself, you almost always can.

"What's this Lewis Carroll drag *you're* in, by the way?" Sam says, lifting a lock of the hair down my back and twitching the collar of my slightly schoolgirl blue velvet. Aurine had a fit when I put it on instead of the nifty she'd bought me. Be yourself, she said—it's time. And it is. But they'll never learn that I can't do it here.

"A tribute to your childhood?" Sam asks. "Or saving our feelings?"

"Smart, aren't you." It's a tribute to them all. Be myself like we *are* on the outside? It would never go. They'd be shattered. But I know how they think I am—or hope. "In breastplates and a see-through, Sam? You think that would go, here?"

"We-ell, let's not think how."

The laughing begins with me, then seeps over to him. Someone passing—is it the Barrymore butler?—grins at us and pours us more.

"Queenie, tell your uncle Sam," Sam says. "What's a smart girl like you bothering with college for?"

Can I tell like him? Though he's the man I once overheard Oscar say Aurine had no envy to, I have to be delicate. Sam's had women, but somehow you never meet him except in the gloomy periods afterward. Somehow, I hadn't ought to mention penises. "Sam—I have to learn—why I really want to be a man."

After a while, he looks up, and says "Flatterer." Sam's smart.

So then I can say it to him, "Why do you all really come here?"

He jerks up a sleeve, toward the photos. Am I also supposed to see they don't make dinner jackets like that anymore? "History . . . and a place to go."

Oh Sam, if you would write plays like that!

I must have said it out loud, Father. I'd had a lot.

For suddenly, he's moving the arm, waving it, to point, point, fifty feet and back, from the window where we are. A long perspective. "My God, my God, why bother staging it?" he's saying. "When life will!"

It's the main house door he's pointing at. A great carved-mahogany door, new when the old joint was, it's high enough to carry a torch through. And Aurine is entering it. She's standing there, filling it to the nth. History has to take a back seat.

Such entrances aren't done anymore. Fifty feet of it, slow as royalty, through men who haven't seen her for years, to their slow roar. She has on that dress in her picture. It doesn't show much of her, by present standards. Except to me—what she's done for the sake of it.

One side of the dress is slashed to the hip. Her hips have that line she says has to be like the bottom of the fleur-de-lis. Like mine. Can't be done after thirty, Queenie. She has. "It's not only the weight, Queenie," she'd said, "it's what's in the spine." And in the heart. As she moves now, the rest of her—that smoky gauze, those tiger jewels, those shoulders—is a mist. Through which each of us can see clearly. One corner of her mouth is especially up.

Beside me I hear Sam say, "Fear of fading——" and choke on it. But being Sam, after we watch her disappear, allagazam! into the kisses, and rise again here and there like a ball of confetti on a champagne fountain, he's able to turn to me and say, "Life's done well."

It's what a man would say. I'm beginning to see it's what a man must. But things are still tit-for-tat between them and me; I'm not my aunt yet. So I give it to him. "*And* Aurine."

For I begin to see what makes my aunt tick.

At the height of the muddle—for me—and the romance —for them—is when I begin to. It's when they're taking her pic and mine. Oscar is. And is it only him she's looking at when she spreads her arms wide—not from second-hand Hollywood but from the heart—and cries out, "I love you all. You're all simply beautiful!"

No. For to me she whispers then, "Aren't they! Must you really leave?"

Yes, Auntie. I must. Beautiful as *you* are, the romance here is so thick I can't drink it. I'm my age; I can see the

history of the men. I can see what *they're* envying. They
don't envy us of course, her or me. Or even the girls on
the outside. What is it then? What is it, with them? With
Sam here? What gives all their noble pans that look of
suffering? That Arctic explorer, like he wants the tundra
again. Sam here, like he wants a new tux. Can it be they're
all envying their former, other, better days? Can it be a
man spends most of his life envying *himself?*

And my aunt knows it. She hasn't come here only to
show them how well she's lasted, but how well they have.
She believes in them. Should I envy her for that?

I've an idea college won't teach me it.

Just then, the old butler cries out, "And what about
girlie there? Does she think we're beautiful?" There's a
slide of laughter—and a hopeful hush. How romantic they
are, the older ones! That butler. There must be a hun-
dred-year age difference between him and me—ninety for
him, and a hundred and ninety for me. I have this time
lag. But Aurine's waiting, her eyes shining. Oscar too.
Even Sam. The picture we all make ought to be the one
of the year, any year.

"Oh I do, I do!" I cry. "You're all so young."

A Family Fuss

Pass on to the Family Affair, a low joke at which Oscar
still laughs himself into hiccups. "Who starts all the dirty

88

jokes anyway?" he'll choke, his eyes streaming. "God."
Certainly some providence wants to keep my attention on
penises, Father. And we can thank the Lord it wasn't a
public day at the restaurant.

We're all there en famille, that Monday lunch, and as
usual in some excitement over who the family will be today. The girls of course are the constants, barring long
Indian engagements like Taffy's with her rajah, or other
road tours. Or new members of the sisterhood, which since
the girls are now in their late thirties or early forties hasn't
happened for some time.

Now and then, there's still a stray like Martyne's "sister-
in-law" from Chattanooga; Martyne isn't married, but the
boy friend who sent the girl up and away was, and has
since got her back again, with a note from Martyne: "I
took her to the track, hon, but all that wahoo-in' bothers
the horses. And the men up here like girls with more
teeth."

Or there was Alba's real cousin from Italy, a lovely
chick but not fitted for free lance, who takes one look at
the girls and gets herself married hard and fast in that
New Jersey nitespot advertises it has a "bride's staircase."
You have to start being one of these girls early, I remind
myself grimly, or it doesn't take; sixteen is pretty late.

It's the men who make our surprises, in the back of
L'Alouette; Oscar says he wouldn't go through his maiden
voyage toward those banquettes again even for Aurine.
Such a hemming and hawing as goes on among the gents,

over the new member of the family, such peals of intro-
duction from his lady sponsor, who is bound to make him
look bigger in the world he's big in than the other men
are, and all this time the quiet assessment from the other
girls, who are treating him like any family does a new-
born: "Looks exactly like her old Mackenzie, regard the
nose! Mack—remember him?" And how he didn't pay her
bills? Plus among the male regulars their own silent exchange, relieved or resigned. Well old boy—I see you're
still here. And so, you see, am I. We both can still afford
the best.

The girls make every effort to convince them of it. Today, not even Indian summer yet, "not even Jewish New
Year" murmurs Oscar, and only the washday beginning of
the week, there's as much fur at this little Ninth Avenue
affair of forty tables, as there is at Christmas, he says, at
St. Moritz.

First, Dulcy, always our trenchcoat girl, strolls in from
Washington in her new one of shaved seal, that costs
twice as much as mink—nobody here bothers with that
old stuff. No ruffles for Dulcy, except her eyelashes. She's
on the arm of Potto Brown, who the girls say is the sweet-
est of all her rotations, and is called "the Commander"
here, because he's an Admiral of the Fleet.

Next in comes Rudolph, ninety-year-old charter member of the Metropolitan Opera Guild, on the arm of Martyne, who is in yards of fox, and sighs contentedly, after
the compliments, "I just can't give up the baby-doll stuff!"

Rudolph hasn't been a regular for years, but she's brought him, instead of her Man from Dixie, on the chance that Tekla, wrestler-in-residence to the UN Secretariat, might be bringing one of her blacks.

She has, swinging in with that nice turbaned one from Sierra Leone, where those new diamond strikes are. Careless Swede that she is, she's wearing an old evening ermine, cut shorter. "White," she says, shrugging. "For summer. And goes well with black."

Alba's late again; she's always in church, making novenas for some wife. Today she's wearing a little nothing made of what she says is vicuña—it always infuriates the girls when she has to tell them. She never wears fur. Everything on her gets plainer, as she gets richer.

"Your clothes are like higher metaphysics, Alba," says Oscar. "Sooner or later, they'll disappear."

Not Alba though, she'll be there, with a neck like a Brancusi, and a long bod like two of them. Feet? You're surprised she has them. Married keep-the-faith bankers go for her—the kind always interested in winged creatures. "Did you confess me?" she says to them. "Don't forget to."

She never brings them here. Like always, she's with Candido, a package-size panther with double eyebrows and hips like fists, who she claims is homosexual *and* her brother. We pretend like anyway we believe this last. She keeps showing us his birth certificate. Like Oscar says, "Alba is extra-cautious. Candido is a forgery *twice*."

Candido is wearing mink.

Meanwhile, Aurine has got herself and me neatly out of this competition. I, the guest of honor, am allowed a sleeveless sportdress, as a gone chick anyway, on my way to being a college girl. "To dress for the weather——" says Aurine, rolling her eyes as she greets the others, "the last privilege of youth!" I know what she hopes for me, by next summer maybe, if I come to my senses. Suffocation— by sable.

She herself is radiant, in white organdie, and ownership. Yards of both surround her. Who can suspect that the year-long feud in the kitchen has only been settled for the day? Or worse, has come to a head?

"Marcel will cook, *grâce à Dieu*," she's whispered to me, meaning "young Marcel," chef fresh last year from Paris, only learning the ropes here en route to a Beverly Hills offer—but if she lets him "marry" me, which he can't credit isn't in her power, he will stay. And if my dowry is half the restaurant.

I'm intrigued by this; no one's ever wanted me for anything except my looks before. Or for something that serious. I've already obeyed instructions to go in the kitchen and sweeten him a little. "No more than a kiss, Queenie, and don't mention college." He thinks this is my birthday fete.

To Oscar, she's just sighed, "Thanks be to God, Marcel will after all serve."

This is "old Marcel," maître d' from before her time, and present figurehead. Until today, many have half believed that he may be the owner here, and he has never contradicted it. He's standing now at the service door, watching us darkly, not a twitch on his bloodhound chops, his artisan fingers stiff at his side. His boast is that he has never shaken hands in his life.

He is also possibly the only male-male in our world who doesn't want to sleep with Aurine. Though a *crime passionnel* might interest him. She's given him the cut direct, by hiring a chef of his same name. Out of dozens of suitable Jacques's and Georges's in the Paris Register, she's maliciously picked the one to make him "old" Marcel. Out with that one, of course, when he himself buys the place; a son of the Massif Central, and of the greatest food in France, knows how to bide his time. Until today—and that dress—she's led him to believe she will sell.

"Simply super, Aurine!" says Potto. "Is it a tea gown? Or a peignoir?"

It has ribbons, and a train so slight you're not sure of it. She clasps her hands under her chin and bends her head in dowager welcome, to Oscar, who won't mind her success of a day, to her beautiful furred friends, in appreciation of theirs, and to me, as the occasion. "It's an At Home."

Still, she'd have caught on that old Marcel was up to something—who could dream what—if the Lord in his wisdom hadn't sent us a new guest.

We've been expecting her, poor thing—being what she is, and on such an errand, even for a ranee. Taffy has

93

wired: "Coming to Mt. Sinai, for a slight alteration." And sending ahead a companion for her stay. One of her war orphans. "The sweet little Indo-Chinese one, remember?" We think we recall the sad little stick—Taffy had eight. "The only one who's turned out well. Out of all that correspondence! It'll be so nice to have somebody near who's family. Loves America. Or plans to. And will have the key to my flat. Do meet the plane one of you. And don't let the dear brood."

The girls rather fancy themselves as foster mothers. Also gladly cleaving to any request from Taffy, who otherwise reports herself "Still on a pearly cloud" with the rajah—and might someday ask *them* out.

The "alteration," being what they think it is, isn't mentioned, even among themselves. Touch wood. Change is their enemy, and they're all nearing the age for it. Well, you can't lie to God; some of them are there. As Gran said once, when I asked a leading question in that department, "Gynecology's so catching, love. Lower your voice."

"Well, the little one will take Taffy's mind off things," Aurine, the frankest, is just saying. "And you girls can all take turns at her." Since she herself will have the restaurant.

The girls agree, putting on their tenderest expressions—and not yet taking off their coats. Oscar says what those girls won't take off often surprises him.

So when the airport limousine draws up in front of L'Alouette, we're all gathered round the door to meet her.

In the rear of the circle is a fine, positive, UN selection of uncles of all ages, black and white, fat and thin—tall Potto, tiny Rudolph, the beaming turban, hostly Oscar, and Candido, who has taken off his coat—he's a man. And out front for her, a selection of mothers right out of Aesop: a vicuña, an ermine, a fox and a seal. And an At Home.

And here she is, she is, on the arm of Juan, the dazed busboy, who is all we could spare to meet the plane. He can't bear to release her, we see that at once. The limousine doesn't seem to want to leave either; half the heads are out the window. Probably the plane at Kennedy is still grounded, hoping she'll come back.

She's tiny, but molded. Her legs are those Oriental bamboo ones look so well in boots. Gold kid ones, up past what in us Goths would be hips. Above that, a short tunic, in a kind of sheer chain mail. We don't know it's real gold, yet. And underneath it all, pure, matchless—pelt.

On her head, when we get that far, is a kind of frail tiara we know is gold right away. On top of a short bob so nutty simple Picasso would want to investigate. The face is Kwan-Yin, but newer. The pearl on one hand is no larger than an oyster. When she shimmers, she smiles, or vice versa. Eyes by Save-A-Child. And two sets of star-point lashes. And when she speaks, at least to her foster mothers, it's Li Po.

She bows deep, in reverence. "Honowable Wadies." Then twirling round to me with a tinkle of kinship, "Hai, hai. *We* must be same *age!*"

Oh, Oriental manners are the end, aren't they, I signal Oscar. He's not looking. Our orphan has turned to the gents, hands pressed together, head bent, eyes concentrated on a spot of her humble self. She is apparently introducing her crotch to them. "It is *Nym*."

"We-elcome, mmmm," says Oscar, in the most impresario voice recent hard times has had from him. "Welcome, mmm, to our new recruit!"

So how can anybody bother to watch old Marcel? Who is serving exquisitely what we've been told to expect—something new. The young one bears the old one no ill will and has let the maître d' choose the meal. From the Maître's native province. "Today," he says, in his hoarse, rock-candy French, "we are in Perigord." And starting off, young Marcel, through the glass arcade that separates us and him, waves across the sea at me.

But who listens, who watches, who even tastes at first?— when Potto is telling Nym, "Do let me help you with your *l* and your *r* while you're here, I'm an old China hand, haw haw, not very old." Candido clearly wants her to trust her *p*'s and *q*'s to him?

She agrees to everything, and promises nothing. "Oh I am so bad, bad, bad with the alphabet."

"*Cou farci,*" old Marcel says. "*Gooseneck* estoffed by *foie gras et porc.*" After that, a strange strangled phrase from him which nobody pays heed to, under the spell of hearing how Nilowan, half-Thai leftover of a Seoul army officer and an "honowable wady from Kowea"—a sweep

96

of the starpoints here—has become, with U.S. assistance and some foreign travel—Nym. "I have so manee sponseurs!" Nym sighs.

Dulcy rouses. "Yes dear. And do you travel with them all?"

"SOUPE A L'EAU DE BOUDIN!" Marcel announces. "Of the blood-pudding vawter made. Specialité de Carnaval!" And again that half hoot, half snuffle.

Delicious maybe, if a little strong—but we're hanging on Nym's reply. "Hai, hai," Nym laughs, with a blinding shimmer, "Nym is orphan."

Meanwhile, Tekla's man from Sierra Leone is much struck by Nym's pearl. "From Burma?" he says, holding the finger it covers. "I have two, very like. One of course belongs to my wife."

"So luckee, your wife."

The girls by now have their coats off, and knuckle-dusters on.

"I love geography," Martyne says. "When it doesn't get too closee. I'm from Dixie, myself."

Only Aurine has her mind on the meal. She wonders aloud whether old Marcel hasn't made the menu too hearty. Or whether young Marcel mightn't have gone too far with the spices? But for once, she suffers the fate of hostesses. No one is minding her. She's At Home.

"Cepes à la Perigordine," Marcel says, this time soft and insinuating. "Mawshroom with-ah le baykonne, ay le pahrrsley, ay le——" His voice dwindles. Again that snigger.

97

"And with—what?" says Aurine.

"But with the garleek and le grape-uh joos, like always, Madame!" He's surprised she should ask. It is the true recipe, he can swear to it. Or ask of the *other* Marcel. He stands there, his long cheeks haughty with the contempt for human interest that has made him the best maître d' on Ninth Avenue.

But Nym is saying Taffee is the sponsor she loves best.

"You've met her?" Oscar's sniffing the wine.

"Hai, hai." Yes yes, or no no, or my my or up yours as the case may, the butterfly on her head wags just the same. "Nym is ranee before Taffee." It seems they take turns at it.

And that takes care of the poularde truffée, soused in cognac, and the tournedos à la perigordine, sauce Madère.

"This wine *is* very acid," Oscar says. "Or something is."

"From Perigord," Marcel says, "not from Bordeaux." Each time he trots through the arcade from the kitchen, which is glass only from waist-height up, we see him stop and bend over the waiter's station, where trays are rested, salad mixed, wine supplied, et cetera. He runs through again, and comes out redder-faced, with a new bottle. "I have corrected it."

"He's drinking," Aurine whispers. And Oscar says, "Well, why not, but which one of them's buying your wine?"

And Nym says, "Taffee so much looking forward alteration!"

98

"Artelation" is what she says, actually, but who's quibbling? Not Potto, who's raising his brows in that tic tic which jumps his tortoise-shells. Not Rudolph, whose tiny old pan scarcely has room for the distress on it; at ninety, he values this crowd because they're so *young*. And not me.

Up to now, I've been sunk under the pall of my Ninth Avenue personality, of years and years here as a *jeune jeune fille*. Now and then, I wave back, at young Marcel. Who Aurine has reminded me now and then is very good-looking, and on the way to a grand career. Of course don't marry him; she happens to know he already *is*. But I could break down and let him ruin me; it's getting late.

He is good-looking, in that Frenchy sharp-nosed way, and I've reason to know his lashes are even longer than mine, though he didn't even take off his hat. Today's cooking is not to my taste, but maybe I'm the trouble with it. Meanwhile I'm squinting at him, through the same cautious virgin lens I direct on all candidates: In years to come, will I be able to bear looking back at you, thinking you were the first one? Father, I don't suppose there are many such lenses left—and I sure wish mine were rosier.

I blame my background, of course—the same as anybody. And right now, all of it, the girls that is, and Aurine included, are looking glum. They might be looking at a pâté of women's organs, all of which have had to "come out." At a certain age. Which, until Taffy, no man has dared associate with theirs. And this interests me. Women's insides, what makes them common property?

Alba says hushed, "I'll burn a candle for her."

Tekla, who's been eating herself into a Swede stupor, is the only one able to look mortality in the eye. And punch it. After all, she had that rajah once. "He eats yohimbim, it's called, before love. Tell *her* to get some. It works. Or that melon the Filipinos won't let be shipped on trains, it smells so. . . . Come to think——" she says, widening her nose over her dish, "this stuff reminds me of it. *Durian,* that's it." She points her fork at Nym. "Taffy eats some of that, no matter what she's had out, she won't miss a thing."

"This *is* a bit gamy," Oscar says. "What is it, Marcel?"

Of course it's gamy, says Marcel, it's a ballantine of hare. Made with a rabbit of course, what else can one do in America? But he has corrected it.

He is beside himself now, a luminous red, standing in his circle of presentations, his exertion reaching us under his cologne.

We too are steaming with wine, and the strange, dark food. "Marvelous, and a little mad," I whisper to Oscar. "I'm not sure what Beverly Hills will think of it."

For I've made my verdict. "Poor Marcel," I say to Aurine, who answers, "Which Marcel?"

But Potto is just explaining to Nym the double meanings of "miss." And Nym has caught an exchange between

Alba and Martyne—oh, she's fast on the catch—and is asking him what means "having things out."

Tic tic-ing all the way, he explains that too.

"Hai, hai—no!" says Nym. She's put out her hands and is flapping them up down, very pretty. "No no, Taffee is having——" Her chain mail runs riot with the strain of it, whatever it is.

"A lift!" Dulcy shouts suddenly. "That's all it is, girls!" She turns to Potto. "Da-arling, you're such a wonderful translator!" She smooches him all over, mmm, mmm. "Oh, I'm so happy for her. Taffy's only having a lift."

Everybody's happier, all considering. Even Aurine, who's for face peeling, when her time comes.

Everybody also agrees that it's really much too soon, that Taffy has always been restless.

"Cain't think of anything Ah look forward to more myself," says Martyne. "In about twenty years."

"Nuts, her face was good enough," Tekla growls. "What's India done to it?"

Nym is looking from face to relatively perfect face. A little string of hai hai's wobbles her butterfly, turning into no no no. She shakes her pearlfinger in front of each honorable lady—not you, not your face either, nor. Nobody here needs a face lifting. "No Taffee either. She fine."

The ladies stare at her. Where then is the alteration to be?

She curves her palms over two tiny places on herself. "Teets."

And the man from Sierra Leone reaches out a long black finger to her tunic. "But that is real met-al, wooman, that is heavy, that is re-al go-old."

We hang on her reply.

"Hai, hai, yes yes," says our orphan, "and so heavee." Dowries are. She droops her head. She wish from the beginning, to take it off.

From half the table, there is encouragement.

"Customs offiseh will not come heah? Examination is oveh?" We are suah? She goes round the table for reassurance, or round half of it. Potto is suah? Oscar, Rudolph? She spares the ladies, but no one else. Especially not Candido. She's quicker at verdicts than me.

Words make him sleepy. He has to lean across Alba. "Ya safe with me," says Candido.

So, in complete quiet, without a hai hai, she takes it off. She's wearing something underneath—we've misjudged her. Still, getting her home like that may be a problem. Two large pearls are taped to her front in very proper places, one to each. She taps them, giggling. "Fwom Buhma. Weal thing." Then holds up the finger with the oyster. "Taffy say, good decoy. Offiseh will know wight away is oney Jap."

"Burma!" Potto jumps as if struck from behind. "Dear me, I know what they do there. Their smuggler's tricks. My dear girl—if by chance you've swallowed any. Or——"

"Translate any more, Potto," Dulcy says, "and I'll turn you in."

Rudolph, with tremoring hands, is trying to pick up the tunic. Not for the gold of course; he's rich. Martyne has to help him. "Fourteen carat, at least," she says. But Alba is the disdainful authority. "That soft Oriental stuff. Twenty-two."

So there we are with our orphan, when young Marcel, holding high the tray, and flame-throwing me glances—I'm glad to catch somebody's—brings in my cake.

It has all the sweetness of France in it, I'm sure. It's made to be ruined. And enjoyed. It has my name on it. And it's in the shape of a heart.

"Speech! Speech!" Rudolph quavers. He loves them, like opera.

"Oh Rudie," Martyne says fondly, "you're such a listener!"

"Toasts first," Oscar lifts his glass of another wine old Marcel has just poured for us. "To——" He looks round the table, and then grins at us. At Alba, Dulcy and Martyne in unholy alliance. At our golden girl. And at Potto, Candido and the man from Sierra Leone—each clearly weighing what will be the best action for a lone wolf who is unfortunately accompanied. Oscar is trying to do the impossible—sum us up.

"To college girls and other orphans," he says finally. "And to Marcel and Marcel."

We all drink to us. This wine tastes fine, maybe because this time there's no food with it.

"Well," Oscar says. "This one's all right."

"A dessert wine of *their* country," young Marcel the chef says, lifting his glass. "Only good one they've got." He refuses one of Oscar's cigars with an air of preferring to flame only toward me. "À mademoiselle." I'm pleased to see he looks at Nym only politely. And dubiously.

"Et à—mademoiselle?" Apparently he's never seen pearl tits before. Maybe he will again, in Beverly Hills.

All this time, Aurine's been sitting there, in her yards of Toulouse-Lautrec. She's taken one of Oscar's cigars, and she's smoking it. She tells me afterward it's her first. Though she's not blowing smoke rings, you would never know. "I had to do something," she tells me later. "I knew I was in the presence of God." But out of respect for his mysteries, which aren't yet clear to her, she doesn't say a word.

When she does this, she doesn't have to. Soon as Marcel-the-younger's eyeballs begin to smart, from the smoke that seems to be coming from hers, he says "Madame is not pleased?"

She speaks slowly. God may be prompting her, but his enunciation isn't quite clear. "It is being suggested, you get a cut on our wine."

His jaw drops. He does of course. But she's always known that! When the head of the kitchen purchases, that's his right.

"But today, I choose them personally," he stutters. "All except this one, the Monbarzillac."

"Hélas." Aurine's voice seems to come from her stomach.

"Maybe it was not the wine." It was not, she said later, I
already knew it. But how can I say what God and my nose
are telling me? Looking at her cigar, she speaks in the
voice of somebody who has swallowed one. "It is being
suggested, that you take a cut on the food."

God thinks of the right insults, all right. L'Alouette
stands fast, but young Marcel's hat may knock the roof
in.

Then we hear that sound, that same sound from the
other Marcel. As Oscar says later, it's the combined sound
of what all the headwaiters in the world think of the
customers—comprising a snigger, a belch and a fart.

From then on (as I tell Sam Newber later) though the
message from above isn't clear to me yet, the stage directions are. Everything goes off—Boom!—in a different direction at once.

The chef, hunched over the serving table, is dancing
from dish to dish, screaming *"Crapaud! Salaud!* What he
has done to it?"

And dish by dish, old Marcel answering in a deep, wine-
dark monotone, is authenticating it:

"Soupe à l'eau de boudin? *Oui!* I pee in it."

"Cepes à la Perigordine? With the garleek, and the grep-
joos? *Oui!* I pipi in it too!"

"Et le poularde!" he shouts. "Le cognac? C'est moi!"
He informs us he's been drinking since yesterday, to in-
sure himself a supply.

Young Marcel the chef is an old Marcel now. He has

his hat off—showing a head shape I could never go for, and is hoarse as a frog. *"Et le sauce Madère?"*

Old Marcel nods, his chaps hanging. He is weaving.

The chef turns to Aurine. "Madame, madame, made with Spanish Madeira, the 1945."

Old Marcel is young. A devilish grin splits his face. *"Oui! Oui!"* He pounds his chest. "And with me, Marcel Boulanger, nineteen oh five!"

Just before the chef hits him, which nobody blocks too quickly, he passes out. As the two busboys drag him to a cab, he rouses. "Not the wine. Tell her, the food yes, and why not, my heart is broken. But if the wine is off, it wasn't me. What kind of a pig would do that to good wine!"

It's Dulcy who starts the giggling. After a bit all of us are at it, even Aurine. All the women, that is.

The men are just sitting there. Are they queasier than us, when it comes right down to it? I doubt it. It's just that whenever the shit hits the fan it's us who are trained to squeal. I wish women wouldn't do that; it doesn't mean a thing. All it means is that then the men can be embarrassed for us. Though we're the ones who end up laughing. I turn to Oscar, who's got an odd look on his face, like the rest of them. On his face I recognize it, sheepish as it is. Why, he's proud! "It's true," I mutter half to myself. "A woman would never think of doing it."

For the first time in my life, he puts me down. "Queenie —it's even truer a woman couldn't."

Just then Rudolph comes quavering in. He's been to the bathroom; he can't get in. Nym and Candido have locked themselves inside.

When they come out, she's wearing his mink.

Then—why, suddenly, it's all female-solemn, and the men who are grinning. Those kind girls are determined not to let Nym go home without company. Theirs.

"To that large, empty flat," says Alba, casting up her eyes.

Dulcy says, "With that large, empty bed."

In fact they're planning to babysit her, round the clock. For after all, what is the main characteristic of an orphan? She's alone.

When they finally leave, everybody is escorting everybody, it hasn't been decided where.

So we three prepare to take my cake, and go home.

In the kitchen, the chef, his head in his hands, turns in his notice. "How is one to cook in this profaned kitchen? With two sets of dishes, like the Jews? No, Madame, I have been spitted on the soul."

"Not spit," Oscar mutters at me, but I won't play. I'm a bit off him. For it's struck me, with a great thud, that it's not only for love that Oscar keeps me and Aurine. It's for amusement.

Meanwhile she's convincing the chef—in French—that his soul is curable. "Expensive. But I'll pay." So she re-hires him for more salary, and a new set of dishes. She says nothing doing though, to any bargain over me.

Though she might have asked me first. "No, no, Marcel, how could you ever think so?"

It's the wine situation all over again; she always knew he was married; now she's using it. "How you think I could give this pure young girl to a—*bigame!*"

Oscar translates in my ear, "Bigamist."

The chef looks up at her. "Why you always call me Marcel, Madame? When my name is René."

Aurine says later it's one more argument for the existence of God.

And the day's not over yet. In fact, it's only suppertime.

We're home, we're already set for bed—or Oscar's saying I ought to go, just like years ago—when we get the call from Martyne.

To be brief—from Martyne who never is—the party ended up at Alba's. All except for Rudolph, who thank God went off to the Met. "He has never missed a Monday," says Martyne. "Then Potto and Candido, they have such an altercation!"

"A what?" says Oscar, holding the phone so we can hear. "Are you sure you're pronouncing your *l*'s?"

"Oh, a fight then, and balls to you, Oscar Selwyn."

Actually she's laugh-talking so loud that Aurine and I can hear even before we scramble upstairs to the extension.

"A real ball-bustin' fight." She seems to have balls on the mind. "During which *fisticuffs*," she says, "which Potto loses, Dulcy leaves."

"Always a mistake, to leave," Martyne says sagely. We know it's one she never makes. Meanwhile, she goes on, Alba and Nym have fled upstairs, away from the violence. "At least that is the interpretation that is taken," says Martyne, all Southern nice-nelly again. "At first." Until Candido, the winner, goes upstairs after them. "And finds those two girls naked as jaybirds. In the sack."

"Never!" Aurine says. "Not Alba." What she means is, not any of us.

"Wait," Martyne says. Seems that whatever else Candido finds under the covers sets him in a rage she can hear three flights down. Maybe he isn't Alba's brother, he's yelling, but he isn't queer either, he's going to settle everybody's hash all right.

"Alba throws him out," says Martyne. "A guy like that is *dangerous*. And she can always get him back."

"Just what did he find under the covers?" Oscar says. Martyne says, "Wait."

Twenty minutes later, she says, Alba's tipped-off banker arrives—to pray for Alba, and throw her out. What do you mean, Alba says to him, it's my brother who was after Nym here, as Martyne will tell you, she was here all the time, you know Martyne.

"An uncalled-for crack," Martyne says. "Which she'll be paying for."

But you always told me your brother is queer, the banker says.

"Hand it to Alba," says Martyne, "she never makes a move she caint prove." Martyne stops for breath. "So once she *does* prove it; she tells Nym and I to leave. And when we do, there they are—she and that banker—down on their knees. By the bed of course. Prayin' for Candido."

"Hold it," Oscar says. "Over the telephone, all this action's too much for me. Where are we—genderwise? And Martyne dear, where are you phoning from?"

She's stopped laughing. "Whah—ahm baby-sittin'," she drawls. When she turns that Southern, it's always the same reason. "Lahk always. Oney Ah don' often get to do it for somebuddy so young."

"Martyne!" Aurine, beside me, is whispering it. "That Nym is a menace. Get out of there, quick!"

"Hon, you know how hard it is for me to leave places. It's psychological."

Aurine is almost in tears. "But *cherie*—we're *straight*."

"Hon'chile," Martyne says, so slow and golden. "We girls *all* are. Three times a day. Ain't it wonderful!" Then her voice drops to its natural. "And if somebuddy else needs a lil bitty *extra* straightnin', why I'm capable." Then in a whisper. "Those two pasted-on pearls were kind of needed—get it?" Then she hangs up.

Downstairs, we find Oscar whooping and slinging his two-fifty avoirdupois around like he's trying to slap his own back. "Don't worry, Queenie," he gasps out. "Laughter is good for the heart."

And I'm laughing with him, again; I can't help it.

Because by then I get it too of course. And a hai hai hai. Nym is a boy.

Aurine is slower to get it; her genders are always so firmly fixed. Then her smile spreads, like for a christening of male quintuplets, like it does for males anywhere, including the Deity. "Trust God."

But hours later, I'm still thinking, "Not on your life! Why should I? Who sez?"—all the things you do think when you're up to here with your own background. Which is seeping slowly away from you. That's the sensation, and it's terrible. All the mother's milk and backchat you've been raised on, slowly curdling. Like your blood's running away from what you are. And you still have to go on being it.

"Don't brood," Oscar says cheerily, having his midnight snack at the kitchen counter, "or we'll have to get *you* a sitter."

I can't smile back. Not even when Alba calls to say next week's send-off for me is still on, her prayers have been answered: on a promise to the banker—to go to a doctor —plus an exchange of large checks all around, Candido is allowed back.

"Well, good night," Oscar says to me, his arm around

111

Aurine. "Au 'voir, Marie Antoinette, if that's who you're being; you're pretty enough. But it's been a hard day."

"*Cherie*——" says Aurine, "you have a pain?"

I think so, but how can I tell her of all people where? Or from what.

"Oscar, she looks like a cow getting ready to butt," Aurine says nervously.

"Calf," Oscar says. "A Marie Antoinette calf." As they go out the kitchen door, he blows me a kiss, and points to the box on the counter. "Let her eat cake."

An hour later, I'm still there.

So this is envy. In the heart of the female. It's a kind of pure feeling, Father, like maybe that accidie the church says sometimes comes over the saints? Like a hole you drop into, from which to see other people's sky. A prison is as pure as anything, I guess. Only I never see my gender as a prison before. I'm into it deep and sudden. A silly chick, sinking from the weight of all her skirts, into the bog everybody told her was there.

And I know what they'll counsel me. Pull those skirts over your head, baby, and just show that bog what you've got for it. Now that you accept the true position of women in the universe, put the best bottom on it you can. Set about learning the *positions*. It's all going to look different to you, dearie, once a man gets inside those skirts.

So it will. Why else am I dragging my feet? There's my cake on the counter, like my virginity. I open the box. A pink-and-white sugar tit with a large *Q* on it, maybe for the largest question a girl can ever ask: "What have I got? What haven't I?"

Answer, from the baritones: "Get laid, girlie. Q-uick Q-uick!" You don't save a cake, you eat it. You don't cure virginity, you end it. And you can't end it and have it too.

Not that I plan to. In our family, a maidenhead's not much of a prize, more of an impediment. Which you have to make the most of. The girls' viewpoint is: Take a good look at the one who's removing it. Every time.

I feel better already. Chewing a piece of René-Marcel's last tribute to me, I feel almost fine. Anybody's background looks absurd, if you have to spend a whole day with it. Especially at the Alouette restaurant.

Too bad of course that God, obeying Aurine's demand to give me her looks, didn't slip in her temperament as well. But that's the deity for you. He's fixed it so no matter what's in our respective hearts, the answer's much the same for both of us: "Take a look at all those lovely men!" Especially since in my case, chances are one hundred and ten percent that the person removing my impediment will be one of them.

So, I just have to hope that college will be different from the Alouette on a private day.

O René-Marcel, today did I see the true theology of the world? Or the true position of women there? Or only how thee differs from me? Not necessarily vive-la. But nothing to do with the shape of your head.

For there we women were, René-Marcel, and there you

men were, a Ninth Avenue motley all of us, but is gender
any classier at the Ritz? And there I am, thinking. . . .

Why is it a woman never feels her organs belong to
herself alone, even while she's sitting there? Why does the
gossip on her insides belong to the world?

Why is it, no matter what kind of mischief one man
does with his organ, every other man takes solemn credit
for it?

Why is a penis such a *serious* thing?

Why else except that we have to take ourselves on hear-
say—for what a man makes contact with every day.

O René-Marcel, we sit to pee. Thee stands. Exposed.

It's no wonder every man is just a little queer for himself. Even Oscar.

So take it away, theology—take it from there. For every
man is a little queer for himself? And God is a man? . . .

I am just hotting to this theory, Father, though not at
all pleased with it, when I hear what I'm not hearing, in
the house. Quiet. Or the sound of the house door shutting.
Oscar didn't go home. And now I'm hearing what I'm
hearing. By the two-hundred-pound rhythms above my
head, never heard before in that bedroom during my lifetime, Oscar is spending the night. Oh the darlings! They
are trusting the theology of the world to me.

Cake makes me think clearly. By the time I've eaten
the whole *Q* on it, I'm seeing certain flaws in the argument. And by the time it is calmer upstairs.

Certainly God is a man. Women can't seem to bother

with the job, I don't yet know why. But is he really man's ally? Is God really as queer for men as they are? Or are we women just drinking their pee?

Well—it's almost dawn before I resolve my answer. When it comes, it's a clincher. Envy's like indigestion really. It makes for a very intellectual crotch. Mine hasn't interrupted for hours. But around five, there's a last little night music upstairs.

Sleep sweetly, my elderly darlings. Rockabye. Rock in peace. Your Queenie is back in her background. At least for the night. Envy is off beating some other poor female's meat.

But when you get up, you two, maybe late subway time, take a yawn for yourself, and a good look at all those heads in the street down there, streaming by on Fifty-Seventh. Not head heads. Just plain heads. Heads! and tails. Take a look at the whole teeming rocking giddy-ap eye-O planet.

Me—I don't trust God enough yet to believe in him. I don't know what he has going for me. Personally, he may have it in for me. But until I know for sure, I'll keep asking myself what may get to be my favorite question. For, look at all those people down there! Look at China, Africa, Japan, Levittown! Look at our old joint. Look at *yours,* Father. People, people, people, people, PEOPLE! All the fucking people.

How can the head of such a place be a dirty old man who digs boys?

But just in case—and just in case He plans to turn up at Alba's—I'm bringing Schubert Fish.

The Bye-Bye Blowout

Oscar says Alba's house is a satire on the rich.

Since the girls don't have too much humor, they get pretty glum when they go there. They have to go, of course. If you're pushing forty, nowhere near the Hope diamond class but never sleep lower than Park Avenue either, then you go to Alba's to see what a girl like you can still get. Or what Alba can. Especially since the men there are all paydirt—men from the serious walks of life. At Alba's, you find out who these are for today. "Better than reading *Fortune*," Oscar says, "and you can eat some of the profits while learning."

It's her food he can't resist; hers is the only place in the world he's had too much grouse. And out of season. Wood mushrooms, fiddleback ferns—what she loves is something the airwaves can fly over in the wrong month for it. "It's her diet," Aurine says. "How else can she scarcely eat enough to keep alive?"

But when the invite comes, nobody regrets. They can tuck in enough wild boar and frangipani foo-foo for a week, if they don't mind the hostess looking thinner than a guitar string in a little nothing made of two or three of them. And meanwhile bone up on what the Dow Jones is doing best on, in one look at the guy she's receiving with.

Alba's the only one of the girls who moves from man to man that much, sometimes even from day to day; she says how can she help the market's temperament? We call all of them "the banker" out of respect for her long-term first one, who she only missed marrying through a change of pope. In return, if you ask, "How's the banker these days?" she'll always answer generously, like "Oh he's in Chile for the weekend, their copper is merging with ours," or "Xerox? I don't see *him* anymore." Oscar says, the air on East Sixty-Ninth Street is now so rarefied you only get the tips on where the stock tips are.

The girls would like to disapprove harder of all that instability, but too much style they want to keep up on goes with it—how can you afford not to know a girl who picks you up at Rumpelmayer's in a Maserati, when you're still paying for your second-hand silver Mercedes, not knowing quiet elegance is passé? And who walks through all the birds who are just beginning to wear whatever— already not wearing it.

It's home where she busts out. Which Oscar says is just what any shoeless girl from the banks of the Tiber, and with a nostril and an arch like hers would do: "There's an emperor's by-blow in *her,* somewhere."

Only where some of her imperial ancestors vomited dinner so they could eat again, Alba vomits rooms. And has
them redone overnight apparently, since though my aunt
and uncle often come back saying the dining room's migrated again, or turned purple according to the latest prin-
ciples, or an Aubrey Beardsley corner is now where the
trompe-l'oeil umbrella stand was, there's never any mess.
Alba claims it's all done because the old mansion the first
banker gave her is plumbing prone—to leaks. She con-
nects this with the house being in exchange for her virginity. When Tekla hooted, *"What* virginity?" Alba replied with great dignity, "My American one." Aurine says
"Alba's very domestic. She's feathering her nest. And that
decorator gives her a cut."

As a kid, they tease me the place is a carousel that turns
around between visits; I keep looking for the brass rings,
hoping Alba will let me have one for being her godchild.
Most of the by-blows in the girls' crowd are; she only
shows us in public until we're five. After that, if we're
ever underfoot when a banker crashes—paying Alba's expenses doesn't mean he has the run of the place—we know
enough to stand very stiff while she straightens our school
uniform and says, "This little dear, her mother's been
like a mother to me."

He has to stand there, holding the little box from
Cartier or the big fur one from Kaplan, and be glad
we're not the monsignor. Who Alba keeps an afternoon
for. Giorgio, the oldest of us by-blows, used to say, "Alba

lives her whole life in a state of qualm." Which she is always overcoming.

We godchildren tend to loathe each other in a tied sort of way. We're too much alike. We stand united though, on not letting that out to the girls. Or to the uncles, who are even more conservative.

Nila's kid, the Nose, now eleven, sums it up neat enough last Christmas. His crowd of boys, which runs from ten to fourteen, is the most depraved I guess, from being all word-of-mouth—when you can really get it up, you graduate. Little girls their own age won't notice them anyway; as soon as *they* fall off, Father, they're after the older boys. And as soon as they can borrow or steal the pill.

"Listen," Nosey says, "it's the girls' livelihood. Why break it to them the style now is give it for free?"

Carolyn, who goes to Little Red, says "And it's our livelihood, you mean, don't you, punk?"

It's not going to be hers, I think.

"Just you wait for socialism!" she says. "Bet you won't get it free though, even then."

I think Carolyn will someday be going to college too.

Nosey makes a noise at her. He wants to be an anthropologist; his term project at Walden is a study of how our national life ignores belches and farts. But I'm betting he goes in business with his uncle, who's a bookie; he's going to be one of those small men who have a fix on livelihoods. "Queenie-so-quiet," he says, "tell us something. Why did so many of the girls have *girls*?"

119

Queenie

It's a fact I think some Nobel scientist should get interested in.

Carolyn perts out quick, "If we'd a seen you first, we'd've abort."

Maybe she'll be the Nobel scientist.

Meanwhile she's in love with Nosey, kid style. And Nosey is in love with me. Our tie being also that we both miss Giorgio, the only other boy in our crowd being Tatiana's Nicky, who is already at Exeter, in his uncle's footsteps. Or partly.

The finalist is Deirdre, Sheelagh's kid, whose uncle in the British Embassy sends her to Spence. And whose uncle's wife was presented at Court. No relation of course, but still an influence. "*Les girls* are simply marvellous, don't you think? With the world situation the way it is. Simpully muh-haw-v'lus."

Are we a lost generation? I think we'll all get married out of spite.

So does Schubert Fish. Who says he might be willing to marry me for it. I bring him to Alba's party not because he's as handsome in his way as any of us, and probably as rich as the richest uncle, but because he's impossible. Like that whole shebang when it's really rolling is likely to be. And because I haven't altogether forgotten about God.

Schu's at my school, my same age, and our bond is that he too comes from doctrinarians—rich radicals. His parents got married under protest, and have continued it. Schubert has never been baptized, or inoculated for anything; he's eaten health foods all over the world, following his father's art collecting and his mother's swamis, but has never had a cup of coffee. In all civic respects, he's a kind of Jehovah's Witness. Though the Fish family don't believe the world will end until the family deadline— which Schu says will be when he's had a hundred women, his mother has attained all a woman can in Mahayana, and his father's found a lost four-by-six canvas of a very scarce painter called Bonington. Schubert has also never been registered for the census, or pledged allegiance to the flag. They never touch money; you have to pick his cab fare out of a pocket the valet puts it in. Schubert has a custom-made pocket in a peculiar neighborhood, just for the girls. I think he'll make his deadline quicker than the others. His middle name is Hegel, and if he goes out of the country again he'll have to sneak back; he's never been vaccinated.

He goes along with his birthright he says, like anybody —until it begins to itch. "Then I told them—send me to school like other kids. Or I'll drop out of here. That did it. Dropping out is *their* bag."

Only it's supposed to keep him and them more in than any of us.

And it's with him I make a real feminist mistake. I tell him my recent thoughts about God. He then makes a male chauvinist one. When I talk about God—he thinks I'm talking about him.

All I see at the moment is our field trips for film class

begin to involve a lot of transport. "No, I've seen that," he'll say. "Let's hop on down to Eighth Street." So when I decide to take him along to Alba's, all I have to say is, "Someone's giving me a party. Wanna hop a cab?"

Up to now, Alba's front door was dependable. It stayed oak. But tonight it's port-wine color; the whole house-front is pale green wash, with a line of potted pink hyacinth straight across. Live ones, and fresh. I say, "Alba's cut from the florist will feed us all."

Schubert's never been home with me. I never bring young guys there; Oscar and Aurine always *look* at them.

And outside the home, none of us talk family, no matter what the family thinks. After puberty, you're not even ashamed of them.

But anybody coming plonk into Alba's will need some commentary. In good faith. So I say, "She never changed the door before; it must be that psychiatrist. Candido's. He and Alba took the banker's check for it. But Candido finked out and went."

Schubert's too smooth to ask who Candido is; he's got a good background. Once inside the vestibule though, he studies that framed birth certificate. When I point out Alba, who is gliding among her guests in a little piece of silk tied in a sailor's knot, he only says, "If I went and got myself one, suppose she'd like a copy of it?"

When Alba mermaids up to us in that legless way she has, I see at once she's pleased with him. Schubert's a lanky redhead with a high-minded profile, like he's studying to be a chaplain who won't go to war. Front-face, he's even fanatical. Meaning pop-eye. But he does a fair job of convincing himself they're concentrating on *you*.

What else Alba sees is obvious, to a hand like her. The Fish clothes are just as funky as they're supposed to be. Nobody's been allowed to polish the Fish boots. Still, the Fish himself has a certain kind of wan charisma. Maybe it's because his nails are so clean of dollar dirt. Or that he looks hungry and thin in the smart way only money can. Like if somebody told you his people don't want him to go to college but to help crew their yacht to the lower Antilles with a load of forty guests and a macrobiotic chef— you wouldn't be surprised.

Alba isn't. She says, "Don't I know your father, Mr. Fish?"

He says politely, if his father didn't only collect early-nineteenth-century, she sure would.

And we pass on to the brats. My godsisters and brother are in the first room to the left, which is kept strictly mansion-style for changing bankers in, so never alters much.

Carolyn nails Schubert at once, for socialism, and he takes her phone number.

I say, "The revolution'll take a while. She's only ten."

He says we're all precocious here, aren't we, he's noticed that.

I say bastards usually are.

"So many of you?" he says. "All?"

And we pass on.

123

Queenie

Passing on seems to be what Schubert does well; he's
what Deirdre's mother's lord keeps telling the papers the
British nation is: unflappable. What you have to watch is
when this sort flaps, but I don't know this yet. I'm beginning to like him for it—that chipped Vermont granite is
really pretty pretty from the sideburns side—and to wonder if this, *hélas,* is *it.* Deciding if it is, I'll get it to close
its eyes. Or close mine.

By now we're at what was called the pumproom the
year Alba bought cherubs, and still has a ceiling of them,
but is the soda fountain this year. Meant for the brats,
who of course won't touch it. But the European-style girls
love it, some even dress for it. Petine Esterhazy, Carolyn's
mother, is drawn up to the bar in gigolo-check bicycle
pants, and a blonde wig with braids. Nosey's mother's head-
dress is the same, but she's still a natty size six, in something made of plastic funballs, and inner space. I'm surprised at Dulcy, until I recall she gave up Potto after our
last blast, for Somebody Southern at the Pentagon. She's
in a see-through Mother Hubbard, tending bar.

They all look as if they're posing for *Elle,* and of course
they are.

Schubert is struck.

"They're not precocious," I say. "They're all twenty-
nine."

"Mamma dear——" Dulcy says to me, leaning over the
bar to him, "kin I touch?"

Schu says "What?"

124

Passing on, he explains he's not nervous with women; it's just he's still so germ-free he has to watch his immunity.

Outside the birdcage room, my favorite, I say "Go on in and tell me is it still there."

He calls out it is, canaries and all.

"No parrots, see," I say. "So no psittacosis."

After we kiss, tongues and all, he says, "I've never even had a *cold.*"

Outside, we bump into Martyne, who cases us quick. "Y'all heard where Tekla is? Flew down to see your old friend Giorgio. She's gonna handle him, his first fight."

I say "Giorgio is a postcard friend." No special germs in that.

But while Martyne puts out for Schubert and I let her, I'm sad. Not for Giorgio. I trust that bo. If his motive is to ruin his beauty, which I think it is, even with a mother like Tekla in the ring, he'll manage it.

I feel sad to find I'm the kind of person who feels sad. But in a happy person today, isn't that encouraging?

On the general level, that's how I analyze it. On the personal level, I can hear Sam Newber's crack—"Half a woman wants to get laid; the other half only wants to talk about it." But shouldn't that be afterward, not before?

With Sam of course, it would probably have to be during.

Meanwhile I see Schubert thinks Martyne, in white pants and her hair in a baby's barette, is very clean. She

125

has the smallest tits that can still be waggled up at a man. She's saying she knows his name, she's musical.

I say, "Uh-huh. Next time I'll bring Jack."

"Who's he?"

All those old men make her gullible, in the end.

I say, "How's Nym."

She's a sport though. She grins at me. "Oh, she flit. And I do mean flit. The rajah had a hurry call." Then she catches sight of little Rudolph. "Pore old thing, he's heading for the throne room again. Y'all looking for your aunt and uncle, that's where everybody is. It's those eats."

I see germs have come up in Schubert again; I'm getting to know that look. And that faddists will always tell you what causes it. He admits the throne is what the toilet is called—diet does it—chez Fish.

"Oh no, it's a real throne," I say. "A present from Thailand. From a member of the World Bank."

And suddenly I'm happy, happy again. Any little bit of life takes me so far. Think what college will do! Talk or no talk, I mean to confess myself to myself all the way. Who else is laughing?

In the throne room, Oscar's sitting on it; he adores any chair can really carry his weight. Aurine's nearby, flirting with a guy just enough to show she's besieged, but standing. When we two come up, the guy fades, but since it's Deirdre's lord, first bowing deep to my aunt. And even deeper to Oscar, who gives a gloomy wave.

This is because he's eaten, and knows he will soon eat

again. I would like to tell him he looks like Henry the Eighth just about to toss the chicken bone over his shoulder in the bit from that old movie. But to Oscar one only quotes legit. So I say, "Your Highness, may I present Schubert Fish?"

Sure enough, Oscar and Aurine both *look*. So before the amenities can take a real grab at everybody, I drag him away again. To the table. On which God, moving mysterious his pinkie at Alba's caterer, has caused to be placed in front of Schubert the forbidden fruit from maybe three fast airliners—including caviar in a swan carved of ice.

And all around us is the lovely throng. They're busy; they're not looking at us. People are loyal to youth though; they'll remember us in a minute, if we make a move.

"This is some do," Schubert says. "Just to send somebody off to college."

"Oh, I know," I say absently. "It's just that none of us have ever gone to college before."

I'm feeling sentimental. I know all along, you see, that these parties aren't really for me. On the girls' side, they're all the weddings our crowd won't be having, rolled up in a ball with some leftover christenings, or some that got stopped cold at the abortionist's—it's too late here for the pill. Or the girls were too early. Bye-bye, bye-bye, Background!

Schubert's saying, "My father has a margravine looks a lot like your aunt."

"What's a margravine?"

127

"A countess of the Holy Roman Empire."

"Where does he keep her?"

"Why—on the wall."

To my mind, exactly the sort of girl a man whose wife's trying to be a Buddha would have. Particularly if all he eats is infertile eggs.

And isn't Schubert exactly the son?

Just then, inching me toward the table, he jostles Candido, in apache drag as usual, who swivels round at once, not even looking at him, and snarls, "Wanna fight?"

Schubert has his arm on me, but his eye on the swan. "No."

Baby, do you have to be radical, to say it like that!

"Neither do I," says Candido. "That doctor is turning me fag."

When he slinks off, Schubert leans down to me. "Who's he really?"

I speak the truth, which is seldom a help. "Alba's bodyguard."

He says he saw at once she has the imperial full lower lip. "I see you do too."

He's his father's boy, if that's all he sees. With what I'm wearing. But I'm looking at my aunt and uncle, who Rudolph is now taking a picture of, squeezed together in that chair.

I know that chair from childhood; it's a religious article, so never got thrown away. It's an Oriental gilt one, the kind made of mixed monsters. You sit in the coil of the snake. A boa constrictor, whose head hangs intimately over the occupants.

They look beautiful there. Sad. That's a dragon's arm dear Aurine is leaning on. The jaw an inch from dear Oscar's neck is a crocodile's. Oh bye-bye. *Bye.*

And Schubert says in my ear, through what smells like his first spoon of caviar, "Just where are you people in exile *from?*"

I mean to turn on him savagely, how dare this snot laugh? Instead I choke up.

Parents! Or aunts and uncles, Father. How can we tell them they're all in exile forever, from us? "Parents," I say. "You know how they are. They still have to think they're royalty."

After a while, he says, "See why they call you Queenie." I never give it a thought.

What I must, must remember from now on is that *not everybody* LAUGHS.

I stand there myself, eyes misty, for I don't know how long. I'm watching the uncles, a gamut from chimps all the way to Oscar, from the Champs Elysées to the Ginza, and never forgetting the Avenidas of the Americas, including Wall. For them this is still solid glamor, hip to thigh. And the kind you can't take home to Mary. It's true, I think, nibbling a swizzle stick. We just know a lot of people who always look good.

As the glittering gowns pass Schubert in gobs of perfume, and the scantie-pantie ones, I can see he thinks so too. Faddists show excitement like anybody else, Oscar says later. "In terms of the original sin." And Schubert is tucking in. Pheasant pâté, quail eggs, bear borscht, glog with goat cheese, and those Bath Oliver biscuits. But it's me he's looking at.

I'm not eating much; I'm feeling too grateful again. And though I'm too old now to have orgasms standing up in crowds, Father, it's still dangerous. Unless I want to stand up with Schubert . . .

I can see everybody's wondering if he's it, and resting their opinion.

He keeps me identifying the food for him.

I have to admire him, he only founders once. "What's *this* I've got?"

I haven't the heart to tell him. Not directly.

"Aren't you eating anything?" he asks, not really caring. He has a small, macrobiotic mouth.

"No, I feel kind of funny," I say, watching what's going down it. Alba gets them from Japan. "Like a bumblebee in chocolate."

I do rather. A live one, ready to zoom out of there. Will I let him swallow me—am I that desperate? Every time I think of it, my boundaries come up in me strong. Can't I go to college the way I am?

At last Schubert dabs his mouth with a napkin and stares at me. His nails are still clean, but those eyes are actually half-closed. He smiles at me, a bit of bee still sticking to his teeth. A piney-winey voice comes from them, the kind that comes off the soundtrack when maybe after five thousand frames of film the two of them in bed up there have finally had it. "I never knew caviar was *gray.*"

But it's my little beaded breastplates he's looking at. I suppose some of those beads *are* gray.

Father, if you had to pick one pure-girl sentence, what a man would never, what would you?

I say, "Excuse me, I have to go to the john."

But I can't lose him. He insists on waiting for me in the canary room, which he claims is right next to it. Turns out it is, though I miss one or two other rooms along our way.

"I have a sense of direction like an *animal,*" Schubert says at the door. "Comes of a pure bowel. And a natural-foods fed heart." Then he gives my beads a shake, and says "Hurry up, my little Hapsburg! I expect to lose all three of them tonight."

Lying back on the sofa with his eyes closed, where I leave him, he looks quite marvelous. And as if he knows it. All along, is he kidding me? I don't deny the possibility, even now. I just don't intend to explore it. Is he that experienced boy the grocers and the girls are always looking for? Or strictly pop-eye? It's enough that what the moving forefinger will shortly point out to me—goes for both.

In the harem that Alba's main powder room always is, most of our inner circle is there, and not just because of the beauty aids which are lined up between the Roman

bath and the sauna, in gold wall spouts Alba lets the manufacturers stock for free. This is the time of evening the
girls gather to swap stuff like, "I told her, 'your only room
pleases me is the boisserie one,' and she says, 'Which is
that?'" Or how they miss the bowling alley, and those boys
from Notre Dame Alba used to hire to set 'em up. If you
stay long enough, you can piece the whole house together,
present and past. But not at the moment. Because our
hostess is there. That single knot of hers has come undone,
and my aunt and a bevy of helpers are retying it.

"No, not there!" says Alba. "I'm expecting somebody to
drop by who is very conservative."

I see the stockholders among us shift their chignons.

Aurine says mildly, "Wear an apron then. Or a bib."

Then it's done—a compromise—and they crowd around
me, congratulating. Cautious on Schubert, hoopla for the
outfit.

I see Aurine is very proud of me coming out of hiding.

"Beautiful, beautiful," says Alba. "Look at her. Nothing
but skin and bones."

I say, "Yeah, it's real funky. Truly rotten, isn't it?" I
don't talk teenybopper usually. But all this is getting to
me; if this is what's riding first class, should I hop a
freight? I have this urge not to communicate.

But Alba wants to. Like all the girls over forty who
still wear size eight, if they can't kill us they want to join
us.

She puts an arm around my shoulders, since there's

132

nothing else there. "I don't care how they say it these days, cara mia. Girls, I want to tell you here is one child who goes with God." She gets all wound up about it. Aurine doesn't tell me till later, Candido's doctor is a papal count. "Remember, Aurine? How her first communion I give her a holy medal, saying 'Kiss God, honey, kiss God.' And how she says 'Will he kiss back?'"

"Well, will he?" I hate childhood quotes. "You never said."

Martyne snorts—she's a hard-shell fundamentalist.

Alba turns on her. "I come to this country, with that prize-fighter Pippo, what am I? A fat wop, in curls and fur. I'm not complaining—that's only God for me in Italy. And now look at me." She smoothes down the sailor knot. "*And*—a Rolls-Royce."

Everybody stiffens. This *is* news.

"Ah-huh," she says. "And which I already know enough just to call it 'the Rolls'!" Then she turns to me. "Queenie, with God like he is in America, you have the best chance of all."

Another snort from Martyne; Oscar says that sooner or later, these pugnose baby dolls always turn pekinese. "What this foreigner means, Queenie, is underplay it, underdress it. Keep the guy with the purse strings on peanuts. And take a daily workout with a thug."

Aurine shifts in her chair. She's as patriotic as any of them. But she doesn't like fights.

"Never mind, Aurine," Alba breaks in. "For once in

Holy Church, this Baptist gravesnatcher is right. . . .
Girls, I made special confession today . . . about Candido."

It always fascinates me, how the girls move in waves.
Or things move them.

"Girls," Alba says, breathing hard. "Candido is not my brother."

Will they hit her? Not at all. I see they have faith in her. Which, as her godchild, I share.

"So I *been* to the monsignor," says Alba. "On very conservative advice. Which he don't answer me right, could make it hot for him." When her bosom rises I see she has more of it than I thought. "I'm gonna adopt."

Aurine breaks the admiring silence. "Watch that knot."

Stupid Nila, who's always on mark, says "So your gentleman farmer, that charley from Maryland, got his, huh? I knew it—the minute the tackroom is gone! Gee—all those lovely ducks."

So that's the room I missed. Well, she still has the canaries. And I have Schubert. Who is either waiting, like men do, or having a second helping. Like men do.

Alba says softly, "Shut up, Nila." Then louder, for me and maybe for the Trinity, "I figure if Candy is willing—God ought to be."

She is really so radiant, so faithful, that we don't know what! In which moment she taps the gold wall behind her and a drawer shoots out. I only have time to think maybe for a holy relic, if so too small for a thighbone, maybe a tooth—when I see a little box is being held out to me.

"That old medal, it's too weak for your situation," Alba says shyly. "Here's one carries the blessing of His Holiness himself, not this one but the one in heaven, it makes a difference. And the chain, it's from Cartier's."

And from the girls. Who soon are all weeping to one another. And describing my bassinet. And counting the pearls in the chain.

Nila says, "Queenie, it's like my pearl rosary! It goes with anything."

Alba says, "And before you *do* anything—kiss God."

Unless, after all, *He* wants to kiss Schubert.

Let him. I owe the girls a thank-you weep. Soon it isn't hard. How touching they are, even Martyne! How can I tell them my whole age group underplays it? And that most of us already *are* thugs.

But Aurine knows me best. I can't ever cry without putting in a little for myself, Father.

"Queenie, is it that boy?"

I can lie to the public easier than to her. "Aurine—if he were *your* first—*would* you?"

They and us should never communicate. It knocks us off our own beeline. Even if it's only four older women in a bathroom, looking back.

"Thanks all," I say quick. "Gotta go."

But I don't get off that easy. It's me made them look.

What a crooked-cozy smile on them!

Martyne says, "Hon—his father that kook billionaire won't *do* anything?"

Nila says, "Billionaires can be very high-minded. Even stingy. Bert hates to book them. Sweetie, maybe you should start lower down?"

Alba says, "She's young, she's ambitious, God will watch over her!"

Aurine has on her cobweb black, which always brings out her happy chestnut coloring. Brightens the world, Oscar says, like a sorrel mare on a dreary Sunday. And takes to autumn's tarnish better than the brunettes. Her smile is her usual.

"And I'll watch Him," says Aurine.

Always believe a believer.

Though as I close the door and lean against it working up my confidence, they're back to norm. I can hear Nila first moaning the loss of the tackroom, then advising Alba to turn it into billiards, which Bert loves! And I hear Alba's double reply. "Ducks I can shoot, ducks I can eat, but he kept score in a book they have—we spend the whole afternoon with that *book*." And then, "You crazy? You think I want Candido should spend his time shooting *pool*?"

Down the hall, there's a faint little glow from the canary room. In the distance, like in a play of Sam Newber's, there is the distant throng. While life dawns on Alexandra Dauphine Raphael.

There could be worse sets for it; I've been in them. The park mall at midnight. The backs of Connecticut cars. A pajama party at Deirdre's, on a slightly crowded terrace with a thirty-two-floor drop. Or a guy's own apartment, hung with those life-size gorilla masks, on Eighth Street.

When I look back on all my experience that isn't experience yet—well, I look back. Looking forward, what's serious? It's my party, and I've already cried at it. And all the doors in Alba's house lock.

Besides, my own music is serenading me. Those breastplates, they push what you've got. Right back at you. The church is right, dressing seductive is a trap. And I'm not struggling. And here is the door.

Does anybody notice rooms much, Father, until something happens there? I don't. What exactly happens anyway, in a room with mirrors all over it, even on top? The pictures are on painted panels between. Risky ones? Sure, but just grotto effects. No Marquis de Sade, or even Forty-Second Street. Nothing modern, nobody even screwing. Just fleeing nymphs peeking back over their own behinds. Fleeing must be about the right aphro for a banker, Father. Disiac.

I guess the Fishes have some banking blood.

And it's my favorite room, I can't deny.

All's quiet there, except in the birdcages. Under their cloths, I can hear them shuffling, in the not quite dark. I'm nearsighted, but I can see Schubert is still sitting there. In a mirrored room there's always a little light. And I see a candle's burning in one of those portable shrines Alba has everywhere. It's on the coffee table, in front of him.

So he's sitting there. And at first I think he's holding another candle between his legs, until my eyes clear. And that's no candle. It's Schubert.

He sees me of course. He's waiting for me. And that's the mindblowing shock of it. *Eerie.* If he'd just've taken all his clothes off maybe, or grabbed me *Wahoo!* any old way. Or torn mine off. I've been through all that. But no, he just sits there kind of drawing-room style, with his trousers open, looking down at what he's got there, kind of doting, like at a rare plant. He knows I'm there of course. Look what I've got here, his smile says. For you.

They say an old-fashioned girl can always find an old-fashioned boy. Or is this God's will on me, complete with wall-to-wall mirror repeats for my wishing to see the male organ plain?

Then it dawns on me, like it does on any girl. I'm being exposed to, of course. I'd've known at once, Father, if it was some poor old tramp behind a bush in the park. But Schubert is rich—at least he always has cab fare. And this is Sixty-Ninth Street. East.

A week later, I'm telling Nosey about it. He's come to declare his love for me, and he's just so cute. And so scholarly. And so sore at me for bringing Schubert. But he says loyally, "Any other girl it would have turned lesbian."

I say "Nosey, if I didn't know you since you slid down Nila's drainpipe, I'd call that a very lesbian remark."

He laughs haughtily; his laugh's getting very mature, and of course his nose has always been. He still has to take care his feet don't dangle, but the buttons saying "Suck!" and "Marcel Proust is a Yenta" are gone from his T-shirt. And it doesn't smell.

"No," I say, "we have to analyze this." I can't wait to. "Exposing himself was Schubert's male *pride*. Plus all those films we were seeing; on a vegetable background that couldn't've been easy. And on his first real meal."

"And with yo-ou," Nosey muggs it quick so I'll be sure he means it nasty. "Poking yourself out at that pervert." He squints at me like an uncle.

"He wasn't perverted," I say. "Not a bit more than any of you, if you could manage it. He was merely being psychological. In his way, Nosey. In his way. If he'd been a great reader like you—Freud, Krafft-Ebing, *Playboy*—it might've been different."

Nosey says low, "Queenie . . . I'm not reading around much, just now."

I say kindly, "I suppose getting it up is always a source of worry to all of you. You wait and see. Oscar says, 'In youth an inconvenience, as age comes on, a pride.' Nosey dear, what you men do or don't do can't be hidden, like with us. So you have to make a thing of it."

139

Nosey says, "Blow that 'Oscar says' bit. You think maybe college will cure it?"

"Oh nuts, it's just a fucking father-image."

With these ten-year-olds, you have to lay it on the line, Father. One nice word about you older people and they're screaming "Fink" at you.

"It's true though," I say, "I can't see myself ever saying, 'Schubert says.' Anyway, it wasn't really me that poor boy was—*addressing* himself to. Not at all."

"You're killing my love," Nosey says. "Just when I was planning a big surprise."

We're up in my room; maybe even at age ten that isn't wise. "Don't you get perverted with me," I say, "I diapered you, once. You want to hear, or don't you? Okay. And keep your hands at your sides."

He folds his arms and stares out the window. "*Address*-ing. Bullshit, in the key of C. Okay, what was he?"

"My penis envy, that's what. What he *thinks* it is."

Nosey says, "Well, isn't it?"

"Now lis-sen here," I say. "Just let me tell you about that envy."

I have to tell someone, I have to start somewhere, it's still like a vision opening out.

"Nosey, it's you men who envy penises. The one you never can be sure of is there. Till it's there. Then of course you admire it. And envy your*self*. Because between times, all a man can do is admire his penis-image. And pretend we do. Penis envy is really *male*."

Nosey has his head in his hands, he has a cowlick. I suppose it's some dose for a ten-year-old; I suppose I could be giving him a trauma, but what can *I* do?

I feel awful for him of course. But great. "Honest, Nosey," I say, "Our feeling is—we just want to borrow it. For where it *belongs*. But I just can't locate any feeling in me that wants the silly thing around full-time."

By now I know I'm being a prick, Father, but who can blame me?

"For a personal possession?" I say. "To play with and treasure in private? Nosey darling, what's a treasure which is neither a secret, nor sure to be there when you want it— or out in plain sight when you don't? And what a hell of a nuisance, if I just wanted to take a walk!"

Nosey says through his fingers, "I walked up here."

"Well——" I say, "all I know is, the minute a man is sure of his treasure he has to hide it in mine."

And he lifts his head. That's what he came to tell me, he squawks. "I can get it up! Queenie! I'm not precocious anymore!"

Here's where Father begins to say maybe my life and times are gone beyond what a local man can handle. Especially for a girl who ever since her first communion thinks she can bang any time on his study door. And who thinks she can have all the joys of confession without the pain of it. Confidentially, he's mad at me because I won't go in

Queenie

the box. I say, the day they let women in on the other side of it, I will. Of course I never talked to a monsignor before.

Monsignor, where would you go, if a boy got *you* in a grotto where he's sitting with a votive light all aglow on his male parts?

Because from here on in, there are still a lot of religious references . . .

First off, only two days before, that boy and I are at the Frick, in front of "The Education of the Virgin," my favorite picture there. Where the little girl is holding the candle to the book, and the nurse is looking down at her like *she* already knows all the recipes? It's a trick one, but it's really together. The Virgin is like any real girl. Young for what's coming to her. And the light shines right through her finger making it flesh for you. And, Monsignor, do you suppose that reminded him?

The second reference, I didn't tell Father. Some things are more for the laity. But the hierarchy like you probably hears things like this all the time. It's one of the limericks this other boy Giorgio and I made up, *Frigid Brigid.*

No work of art but it says something to a young girl.
. . . *Frigid Brigid remains quite rigid, Even under her own digit, Breathes there the Man or maybe the Midget* . . . Whocanmakefrigidbridget *fidget?*

There. And if you ever think of another rhyme for *igid,* let me know.

Now—go back to Schubert. Because when I see him

142

sitting there like that, that's what starts going through my head like a freight car. Idgety idgety. And right behind it, on and off like a three-way flash bulb, the Frick. Plus a rhyme for that.

Schubert's not doing anything though; he's not really a pervert. I can't even tell whether he's looking at me. Those eyeballs are no cinch to pinpoint. What they're saying to me doesn't need it. "Baby," I'm saying to myself, "will this be your trauma from now on!"

Well, it will in a way. Only, on comes another complication.

I hear birds. And that's the eeriest. Because they seem to be behind me—you know that little shuffling sound they make? Yet I can see quite well, they're all out front. Twenty or so birdcages, and not a tweet out of them. Then I freeze rigid, all right. Because that bird shuffle is strictly to my rear. Maybe like Saint Joan I'm hearing voices, and who could blame her in my case? Or maybe it's me kicking myself. But then, standing very still, in a pause Schu maybe takes for pose, it gets to me.

These birds wear perfume.

Bye-bye nothing! Behind me, I've got my whole background.

I even fancy I can hear Gran. "Dark as the inside of a cow here," she'd say, "Queenie, watch that lollytrap between your legs; this time o' night the mice come in."

I can't hear Oscar. He's only a father-image. And he's said enough.

Even my own little music man has quit. Mum's the word, he says. Or Mom.

Because—by the twenty-dollar-per-ounce smell behind me I've got four live ones standing ready to do right by me: a muguet ingenu, a southern gardenia, a triple essence of tuberoses from the pharmacia attached to the sacristy of Santa Maria Novella in Firenze—and a Joy.

When I get to this part of my life is when Father and I disband for the moment, on a technological argument. Over whether the girls should have gone on standing there.

He says, "For every poor soul who shows himself, there's ten women willing to watch."

I say, "That's unfair, Father, there's that many more of us. And we only want to compare."

He says the pure in heart will take what comes to them.

I say, what would I be doing in his study if I was pure in heart? I only came to tell him why there's no envy in it.

"If you were to show me your*self,* Father, and I looked —who would be wrong?"

It's then he stands up quick from his chair and gives me a blessing for free, saying he'll take the penances. Saying the Dominicans have done all they can for me. It's time for the Jesuits.

So I think, maybe just as well. Father is very pure in heart.

. . . And I don't mind moving up. Though I see even

a monsignor doesn't shut the study door. The view from up here is very impressive though. All those clouds . . .

So is Schubert impressive by then. He doesn't seem to see or hear or smell. He's in the highest state of self-pres-ervation I guess a man can be in, except one. Which he's clearly counting on me to join in on. And I'm giving it the more serious thought.

Not with the girls there, of course. But one waggle of my hand behind me, signaling, "Bug off!" and they would've, I know them. They're only waiting for me to make my value judgment. And I'm thinking, at last Queenie, going on seventeen you poor doubtful titivated creature—you've got it made.

I'm even moving toward him now, breathing hard, like what you do for breastplates, but this is natural. *And Schubert is closing those eyes.* What tact!

And me, I'm exalted. Monsignor, a man without envy of himself is a wonderful thing! But with a light on it, it's a sight almost out of imagining. In such a holy moment, what can a girl do but kneel?

Monsignor! I'm only admiring. And I am a little near-sighted. . . . And you're not nearly so pure-hearted as Fa-ther Detwiler. . . .

So, well, the rest of it is all theology.

Really? I thought maybe the hierarchy mightn't have the time.

So, well . . . we both know the text for the situation, don't we.

145

Sure you do. Pride goeth *before*. It was Gran's favorite.

If she'd been there—Gran had a heavy foot and a low boiling point—would even that have headed him off? I wonder. Because by then, I think that boy knows he has a larger audience.

Maybe he even figures scoring with all of us instead of one will bring the end of the world that much nearer.

Oh men in that state are so naked to the blast, my heart still goes out to him wherever he is—as long as he's not with me.

Because five little prideful words come out of his mouth —and he's ruined. Let that be a lesson to me. Ruined by talk.

You won't have more obscenity here? Monsignor, you're not getting it. Not from him. You have to remember what Schubert has behind him. His whole background.

So listen now. Just listen to the envy of that boy.

"And it's not circumcised either!" says Schubert Fish.

Well, I told you. Four girls suddenly giving out a terrible cackle, in perfect attack like they've been trained for it, it's a cultural shock. Followed by two dozen canaries, miscued by the noise, who are off on what sounds like a mixed chorus of "The World Is Waiting for the Sunrise" and "I Love You Truly."

Ah, a man in the pure state of pride is so vulnerable. You can see it by only one votive light.

The girls stop laughing on the double of course. The birds trill on with a second round of "Sunrise," that's what canaries are for. But one round was enough.

Pride *goeth,* before a fall. And what's worse than the kind of fall you have to stand up and button your fly over?

So now Schubert and I are seeing each other straight. Looking, looking, like we're at the end of a year-long affair. Or over the summer, when you get back to school. He knows I'm no Hapsburg. I know he's no trauma a girl can't get over. We stand there, background to background. As I say to Oscar later, gender's just a ditch with two sides. . . . As *I* say to Oscar!

As I say to myself, still stuck there; Queenie, you can go to college just as you are. Virginity's just a matter of taste.

Then I look behind me.

There they are, the pretty beasties who reared me, their teeth still gleaming with a fearful glee. Four hearts without envy. And times four—a heart.

Alba's face is all smeared with contralto feeling.

And Nila? What's that other stupidity, oozing over her like honey?

Martyne's the mean one, but you can see, even she's got a secret she'll guiltily keep.

Aurine's the one always conquers her laughter first. Leaving her up on her haunches, with that lion face both genders love. Because wherever she is, is the kingdom, the evening's eye. And the aunt with whom you can communicate.

147

She sees I know it now. The secret that keeps women silly. Suppressed laughter. There has to be a real detour around laughter, in any loving woman's life.

So, when I motion them "Bug off!" they go. It's not for nothing I was brought up by daughters of joy.

I guess that, by nature, I come of the same self-confident school: open-face disorder about my civic rights, and a ragbag confidence in the gentlemen. In what they can't do as well as what they can. After all, we're there, so to speak —in readiness. The gentlemen have to show themselves.

So there I am, Monsignor, left with the answer to a simple question I never had the wit to ask. The one you men try to keep us from asking.

What have we women got between the legs, that you haven't?

What have you men got, that we haven't?

I can tell you, Monsignor, because you can't use it. And you needn't look so worried at the door.

You're temporary. We're permanent.

And that's where the ditch comes in.

O Monsignor.

You have the envy.

We have the heart.

And I still have Schubert. Who I see I'll have to help do what he does best. To pass on.

"Oh, Schubert," I say, "is there anything I can *do?* What *can* I?" I mean it. And I don't laugh, until later.

He draws himself up. I see what those eyes are looking at. Sin, Father.

"I'll have a cup of coffee," he says.

I hear later he has three. After which he spends the night there. But not with me.

All the way home, which I sneak back to alone, me, I'm hearing a tinny little tune from my music man, like in three-quarter folk. *I lost my cher-reee, a-what, a-was, a-it?*

So I go home to my deck chair, and spend the next few nights on my rooftop, more or less in the company of a very important personage. Who has looked after me better than I think.

Sure close the door, there's a draft. But I love your view.

Wha-at? Why Oscar's my father-image! Why that would be incest—what a drag. It would be like doing it with you.

Monsignor. Some cherries are in the *mind*.

Oh, it's okay. I guess after those parties of mine, I do feel rather intimate with Him. Father Detwiler thought I meant Freud . . .

I suppose I kind of rushed, Father, when I went back. 'I've got a secret; it's only the world's—but *who* can I tell it to?' That's the feeling. Everybody else I know is so weighed down with gender . . . Isn't that why they keep *you* celibate? . . . And after three days and three nights wrestling with it almost like whoozit in the desert—although this is overlooking Central Park—I wanna tell somebody. That I understand why God keeps on *hanging around.*

What I want to do is dedicate a word of thanks to Him. In somebody's *hearing.* I see by now why all my sessions on cloud-deck, from way back when and no matter to who, are really prayers to Him. But this one is like from the whole female world . . .

So I run over there, bang on the door and slide on my knees before Father can say Succubus!, which he is clearly geared to, or is it Incubus!, and bawl, "BlessmeFatherfor-Ihavesinned"—because that's the formula. And I must've, somewhere.

But right off, Detwiler and I are off to a misunderstanding. Not every girl's confession is about getting laid.

So there it is again. Envy. Right in the church.

I say, "That's my trouble, Father. When I sin it's never what people hope. I'll come to you the minute it is, though. I'll even get in the box."

But he's a good man, he hears me out just as I am, only near the end he gets nervous. He says maybe I should go higher than him.

I say, why—when it appears like women are already in conference with the top?

He says certain special sins are reserved for bishops to hear or even the pope; maybe meanwhile I could confess over again some old mortal sin from which I have previously been absolved, he's not too sure yet what my present one is; do I aim to confess or to brag?

I say why not both? And whatever I could've been ab-solved from way back then in my childhood, at my age now it might be ridiculous.

Finally he says to come to you and tell you exactly my theology, you deserve as much news and cheer as anybody, and are like the half-head of the diocese. And might even want to take notes on it.

Which is all right with me. When women really level—it's not bullshit.

Okay, I'll watch the clouds. You watch the door.

"Father," I say. "Penis theology is a leaning tower. The education of virgins ought to be left to God."

". . . Whatever else are women thinking of, Monsignor, with all that clutter we have, sends up a flag once a month to remind us as far as coils and wires and power supplies go, we're built like a Con Ed substation inside?"

"Screw those analogies about the bees and flowers," I say, "that's what's almost done for us. Ditto the Amazons, with their bows and arrows, when all their ordnance is al-ready built in. What's a bomber pilot say when he lets go? With a heart full of envy, no doubt: 'I dropped an egg.' "

. . . So I say, "Father, I go to college with some convic-tion. I mayn't know what my own expression inside is yet, I say. "But whatever I am personally, the universe has sure declared confidence in me. Why, Father, what can even a radical feminist do for the rights of females that Our Lord hasn't already done for her, even *before* she opens her legs?"

Queenie

And when she does, Monsignor!

"Now, Father," I say, "I want you to visualize them out there, four hundred million or whatever it is. *The female population of the world.* The entire roll call, all present and answering. All of them lying in front of you with their legs open. But you're a man of God, you can see straight up to their hearts. And what do you see if you are as objective as Him? Not sainthood; He's made that unnecessary. Hearts, when you get right down to them, without carnal covet of any kind. People who have the power plant don't need to have power complexes. Hearts full of laughter, aren't they, Father? Okay girls—snap shut. Stand h-up! And Thank the Lord."

Oh Monsignor, we're helpless creatures, we can't help ourselves really. Why do we have hearts without envy? Because God is for cunt.

THANKS!

T W O

Queenie:
✌ POLITICAL FUCK

NINE WEEKS here at the Hencoop, over fifteen hundred girls—what a life-force!—and like eggs in an incubator, every one of us has grown up.

Chicked!

In fifteen hundred ways, though Oomph says trends are boringly discernible.

Our hair is standing straight up with the electric shock of the new world.

Or the outside one. Or the inside one. Whatever we didn't have before.

Got no time for cloud-confession now, or any of the old kinds; *every*body's talking.

Which Sherry says is great for sanity. Nine times out of ten, if you overhear yourself say something freaky it isn't even yourself.

Any private thoughts you have here have to be strong

enough to be written in prison on toilet paper and sent to the President. And no thoughts are any good here unless you *lay your bod on the line* with them.

Not in the college, not in the country. One hundred million people in the U.S.A. alone are watching us, even when we're not watching ourselves, and everything a college girl does is a significant act. Our indignation is endless, righteous and scrumptious—and nobody said that; I overhear that line all by myself.

Our difference from other good people is that we stand ready to authenticate ourselves in action at any time.

Where our brain goes, our bod goes. Or ought to. To Cuba or to bed.

We come to college to educate.

And the faculty is learning a lot.

And all of it is only fifty blocks from home.

And this is my term paper on myself; the bod comes later. According to who this document gets submitted to.

"Oh, it'll go to a who——" Oomph says, "don't you think we all will?" Both of them are reading it. Sherry says, "Who else? A whom is a Jerk."

Our charm for each other is that we could say "Just like me!" to each other fifty times a day, and yet we are totally different. Like Sherry will say, "Connecticut is the most *American* part of America." By which she means the worst of course; she comes from there. And Oomph, who's from L.A. via Phoenix, will say, "Another goddamn Eastern snob." I'll say, "Girls, whatever, just don't let's be doc-trinaire."

Unless we find a doctrine we like of course, which each of us apart from the others is secretly pursuing.

Secret here means something we all know.

Meanwhile they're trying to cure me of saying "Girls." And it's for sure we're all being cured of something. "Join up," Oomph says. "Smart as we are, they're not telling us yet of what."

Oomph already has a reputation. With the faculty be-cause she is fourth-generation Hencoop, and all of them hellers who have subsided proudly into private life; she says her mother is a little overdue at it but her grand-mother was a grande dame before forty.

With us, she's the author of a four-line poem called "Intro" which one underground critic called the best word on coitus since "Post coitum omne animal tristum est"—and which appeared on the masthead of her school paper all last year.

"My maiden effort," she says. "After that, what that oink calls 'coitus' took over."

Sherry says moodily, "We three all have the fault of language." Having the fault of something is a Christian Science phrase; her great-grandmam helped found the *Monitor*. And she and Oomph have heard a few co-au-thored limericks from me.

"The real truth about college," I say, "is that everybody has a background."

157

Queenie

Oomph's problem is that with every school she's kicked out of she gets brighter and brighter; she says maybe at Hencoop at least the second part of the process will stop.

She says she's the type even if she ends up on a death wish, something practical will come of it, she can't help it; she will probably survive as the head of a large department store which she will totally transform, maybe with the primitive clothing and animal furniture that modern depressives love.

She can certainly regularize any plan of ours by merely listening—and a couple of practical suggestions. At present she is writing one term paper on "Brute Parallelisms in Modern Thought" and another on "The Turn of the Screw," using the modern meaning for Screw all the way. We are helping her with them because she can't spell. But boy-oh-boy, can she analogize. She says so herself.

Oomph's poem is:

> I (eye) am an auk
> Who fucks
> An I (eye)
> Who auks.

So you see she is probably right about "whom."

So here *I* am, happy as a lamb for the slaughter, a member of the most influential set in the school even though it's the largest—not the ones who are *in* but the ones who are *out*. Oomph's mother, who we call Mrs. O. because she hates it but would like to be den mother to us, says in her day the majority didn't give itself the airs of a minority, but we seem to want everything. "Anyway, you're all pretty enough to go around as grubby as you please." Which she really means; Oomph says she's quite far forward. Meaning for a mother, too much.

On dirt—as Mrs. O. bitchily points out, there are still divisions among us. Between the ones who wash under the armpits and in all the private places presumably, no matter how fiercely street-stained their feet are—"and the ones who stink all through for the sake of whatever revolution is for today." Like any stool pigeon, she's half right. Among the first kind, the really classy dilettantes and usually the rich ones, I myself know one who can't go in youth camps or pads—she has to have a bidet. The second class, they have to have everything dirty; even the men they sleep with mustn't ever shave.

Among us three, we overlook the division, which is luck for me. Oomph fucks and washes. Sherry fucks. I wash.

But none of us yet is really political about it. Which makes us farther out than anybody here.

We three get together originally through the college system of pairing a "bright" roommate with a "good" one. Which gives you some idea, Oomph says, of the anti-intellectualism at the root of all college administrations.

When I overhear her say that, I am awestruck. I say, "A minute ago, I wasn't even capable of thinking that thought myself, much less phrasing it. But the minute you said it, I was!" Which is an example of the rate of learning here.

Queenie

"Soon as the pairing's done," Oomph answers, "we can all swap. Along the lines of sympathy the college hopes to avoid."

So she and I let the two cocoanut cookies we've been paired off with go off into the sunset together—two very nice dumb Indianans, who both love school.

"You shouldn't love school," a girl standing near us says, "my older sister did and she got trench mouth."

We turn, and there is Sherry, the filthiest beautiful blonde you are ever likely to see wearing Spanish suede shorts and a rubber life jacket. Or to smell. She has the single next door to us.

So in the end we get a boy we know to axe through the common wall between her room and ours—which the authorities ignore on the basis that in a year or so the dorm will be coed and physically ruined anyway. And there we are, ready to educate ourselves, which from one look around us we already know is the way it will get done.

Then Oomph, always the leader, says, "Let me tell you about myself. Now—my mother——"

Which Sherry quickly counters with, "Don't you mean *my* father?"

And I say, "I'm a bastard, myself."

And pr-ronto, we are friends, on a plane of subtlety which is given to few. Not more than maybe half the fifteen hundred of us. The rest, who are either too stoned or too square, are left for the faculty to educate. Plus a few of those stunned girls whom nobody knows why they

160

are here, especially themselves. These days, the trend in the better universities is: You don't only just go, you know why.

"Shee-yut, I know why I'm here," Sherry says, "I'm in training to be real." She likes to think her name just might be short for Scheherazade, but everyone knows her parents are top-flight account executives in a large ad agency, and the fact-fantasy borderline has been very difficult for her. She can't even wear stuff like jeans, because one of her parents originated the word "sudsable." And the only thing two years with a shrink did for her was to help her remember which. "Guess *whom?*"

None of us three is engaged in blaming our backgrounds. The last generation of backgrounds already did that. Our commune of three is aimed to balance out: Oomph's inborn sophistication; my naïveté—which they both say comes of being brought up on the facts; and Sherry's dirt, which is inarguable. The house rules are: Tolerance for all. And keep the beds far enough apart, to discourage dikiness.

On one thing we are all agreed. The difference between the genders is different here!

It doesn't seem to depend only on fucking.

The switch is that everything else does! Diet, poetry, politics! Some girls won't even fuck with a guy unless he eats the same. Fucking is charity too, just as much as giving your blood to an Ozark child or your kidney to your brother. Fucking is religion—you can slide like a glass bead down the life-force, arms locked with anybody from

Fillmore East. That's a rock theater; I haven't been yet. Even before you do anything, you know all this. Fucking is music too, and ballet and art—it's what you want to make it. But most of all—you can fuck the world.

"The only trouble," Oomph says wearily at the end of one of these night watches, "the word's wearing out; they're gonna have to find a new word for it." And Sherry, who's writing a paper on Wittgenstein, says, "Tish, tish, then it'll be a new *thing*."

"Oh girls, everything's all pouring out for me at once," I say into the dark across the beds. Mine is in that beautiful axed-out opening. Axes in the home! "Education is like something I already knew!"

Except for the classes of course, which can be very interesting if you feel you have to be like that. It's the extracurric which worries us, because it's the part will turn out to be serious.

Mrs. O. is always telling us what extracurric meant in her day: college-sponsored socials and dances which nowadays don't exist here, maybe in the funny papers in the Middle West. She comes from there, and has one of those hard, ovarian voices you can't get away from, that seems to have no connection with the face. Hers is narrow Irish Angel. "Convent-bred and country-club cured," Oomph says. "Draws men to bed or to church, often simultaneously."

Sherry says the voice is the kind says to a man, "Many are fucked. Who chooses?" even when it's asking for a cup of tea; Sherry kind of envies that.

I wonder if underneath it all Mrs. O. isn't a starchy shit, maybe even strict as a wife.

"Oh no," Oomph says. "Poor Mother, she's easy enough in the general business of life. Meal anytime. Date any-where. But she can't help the dust is gathering on her life style."

Sherry says softly, "Your mother would like us to forgive her for her hostility to us."

Oomph says, "Sister, your training is paying off."

This is all because Mrs. O. has developed a habit of dropping in on us, to loll on our floor in her Hencoop 1950 tweed skirt and sweater, drink our wine, and say things like, "My God, we freshmen still had to have a smoking room. To smoke in." It bugs her we don't smoke. Not the cancer stuff.

"You discover all our differences with such zest, Mother," Oomph says gloomily—she hates being approved of, in any way.

And ten minutes later, there is Mrs. O. reading out a headline from the college newspaper, *Omphalos*. "My God, isn't that wonderful, you kids don't realize your own emancipation. Why look, right here after the weekly cal-endar, it says 'Motherfuckers, unite!' "

We three groan, which may seem impolite of Sherry and me. We are bored with language by now; it's such crap. We're not verbalizing; we're happening. But we are mak-ing a communal effort to understand Mrs. O.—which Oomph says is a gratuitous act. And Sherry says goes for her father, too. "I'll never convince him he's not *important* enough for me to understand."

I am thinking of home. "Oh—I wish they all *were,*" I say. But we all know my hang-up.

I have to put all this down in some detail because of the orgy, which I would never have understood otherwise. And because I've been instructed a term paper must be in sequence, even if it is about yourself.

Sherry's father dropped in once, but it wasn't a success; he discovered *our* drop-in, the boy who lives in the dorm basement, in the furnace room right under us. "Why is he here?"

Sherry is sitting lotus-legged on the far side of the floor—stinking from three days in a pup tent on Montauk with a friend; *"Healthy!"* she said when she came back, but though it's well into December by now, she hasn't changed those shorts yet.

She looks up and says, "Howdy, Pap, and what is the Tarot telling us for today!" She takes a mean pleasure, she says, in talking how her father thinks we do—oh, the mean pleasures we take! Because she says he runs right back to the agency files and looks up all her references; he even *uses* them. In his work.

"I find that sad," I say to Oomph later. "Because her references aren't *her*. And he'll never know that." Oomph says, "Will *she?*"

Anyway, at the time he says, "I asked you, what is that boy doing in the basement. He's got a regular setup there—is it *sandbags?*"

"No," she says, "it's cracked wheat. Wholesale, from East Tenth Street, that way he avoids the middleman. We chip in for the skimmed milk."

"He goes to classes for us too," says Oomph. "He's getting our education."

"And sleeping with you?" says her father to Sherry.

What a phrase for it, Oomph says later—it certainly tells all!

Sherry looks him in the eye, she can't wait to. "Not particularly." But what really breaks him, she finds later, is when he writes the administration about the drop-in and gets a stiff note advising him to stuff it; they're having a hard enough time pretending not to know.

After he goes, Sherry takes a shower in celebration, she's really been saving up her dirt for him, and we are relaxing over a little hard study for a change when Cutchy, the drop-in—James Boyd McCutcheon the third or the fourth, he likes to pretend he's too stoned to recall—woozes up the stairs with his hair in an Afro haystack—you could rent it out to people for romance, Oomph told him once— and says, "What was *his* bag?"

"He's my father," Sherry says, and we all sigh, because that expresses it. It. Them. All. Lots of people look like their cars, she says, but Connecticut people look more like them than most. Her father's is a Cadillac.

"Well, he's hopelessly sincere," says Cutchy, meaning insincere of course, you have to know our references. "I gather he's made a career of it. But I hear he paints on Sundays."

165

"A successful career," Oomph says. "How do you think she pays for your milk?"

"Yahm," Cutchy says, meaning yessum, which has a whole lot of history in it. His. "Well, he gives me the idea maybe I should be in the sack with her more for it. Sherry, want come downstairs?"

She saws her towel up and down thoughtfully; she's a waverer. And rarely decides against.

"No you don't," says Oomph. "She's just changed those shorts."

So we're all four drinking the grappa from the Montauk friend's still—we're not much on alcohol but this is nature stuff—when Mrs. O. drops in for her group therapy. She knows about Cutch, but hasn't met him yet. Same for him.

"Meet Cutchy, Mrs. O.," says Sherry. "He's supposed to be from Farmville, Virginia, Prince Edward County, and makes like he's a black albino, but he isn't. He's an albino, but a white one."

"Meet my mother, Cutch," says Oomph, "but watch out for her, she marries role players. Whom she then deflates." Sherry and I know about Mr. O., a tough stockbroker who Oomph says was so deep in his role he was almost natural, and so thick-skinned he lasted eighteen months before he divorced Mrs. O., who refers to him as "still playing the love game." With her. Of course the reason she is hard to talk to is because she is communicating all the time. And very conscious of it in other people.

She keeps following us around, because she thinks we know how. When she isn't denying it.

"Oh you young ones, always phrasing your life before you even *have* it," she says now. "Leading our lives took us *time*."

It kills us she can be so perceptive and then stop. For instance she'll say of an East Village couple, twenty-eight-year-old ex-folkies who keep a headshop-and-dress boutique Oomph took her to, "Must be hard to start life wearing granny glasses, being called your old man's old lady, and then find yourself settling down." But then she'll say again, "We took our time."

Sinister. They're always trying to give us time like an object; Oomph says they find us terrifying because we have lost it, and have no intention of acquiring it.

"Time is property to them," Oomph says. "Twenty years after the bomb—they're unbelievable."

Sherry says, "I *said*."

I'm too old-fashioned on this to do more than gape. Back home the girls are still so bogged down in time in the old way I understand it; who knows, I may even be that way myself? A bomb-virgin, so to speak. Maybe virginity goes all through a person?

But right now Oomph only says, "Don't mind my mother, Cutchy. Her intellect is her thorn."

"Evening," Cutchy says politely. "We are just discussing, do those liberation girls who chop off their hair for freedom really want to cut off some man's balls? Scares me right much, down in my basement."

Mrs. O. says for his sake she hopes they'll stick to hair.

Sherry says, "Oh why do those chicks make such a fuss? If gender's on the way out, don't we all know which?"

"Mind telling?" Cutchy says, though we've been over all this before. He's sore she said he was white. Which is an understandable hang-up for an albino.

It's smug of me, but I never get tired understanding people's hang-ups. My own most of all.

"A woman can go get herself inseminated," Oomph is saying. "And take the future of the race with her. But you can't put an egg basket in a man." She still has her hair though.

I put in my two cents, which is seldom. "Navel to navel, Cutchy—there's more behind ours."

And I tell them what you told me, Dr. Werner.

I say, "Education is really just finding out your thoughts aren't only yours, the faculty says."

"Or even theirs," Oomph says.

"How *is* the faculty?" Mrs. O. asks, like of an invalid.

We look to Cutchy, our representative.

He says, "Ma'am, they're taking us through all the crimes in history, and then asking us what to do about them. Or saying, 'Go do.'"

"Well in my day, they didn't ask," she says brightly.

It's warm and reflective in our room, being so near the furnace room, and I am thinking how much cozier it is to bear the intellectual burden of the world in congress, instead of like nine weeks ago when I was doing it all by myself. And have like a glass of wine while you're doing it, meanwhile stretching your flesh in a new jumpsuit, of which when you brought it home a whole floorful of girls approved. Plus the boys who are staying overnight with them.

Turns out Sherry is having her own thoughts about the comforts here. Being clean always unsettles her. She says, uneasy, "Hang around here, and you begin to feel you could almost do without men."

"Can it," says Oomph. "It's only an hour since you got back."

And I am thinking dreamily what one of the faculty said to me—or maybe to the air—after his political science class; talking to them privately makes you feel like a stool pigeon here, maybe they feel the same. But in the end each side keeps moving to keep the lines open.

"Doctor Werner, you know him, you know what he said to me?" I say. "He said, 'And how are all you devils stewing in your broth?' "

And I think right away, devils or not, yes we're like that here; any of my brethren moves an arm, I feel it in the leg. Youth is the broth! And maybe political science is my major!

Cutchy says, "Anybody hungry?"

Mrs. O. says, "Who is this man Werner?—what a nerve! With what we pay for you to go here!"

And that's it, folks. Whatever they say unites us against them in the end, Oomph says. But I know money is the worst. Especially when you're living on theirs. Beyond a small diamond sold, I'm not, because of a shockeroo of a scholarship, that turned up after I sent in my application essay. But I can feel it in the others, through the broth.

It's terrible to watch your friends close in on an oldie. Who doesn't even know. And to find you almost like it.

It starts with Oomph saying in a silvery voice, "Hungry, Cutchy? My mother's taking us out to supper."

And Cutchy moving in as if he's only any undergrad after a free meal. "You mean she's taking us all?" But like the poor hen doesn't know what he's got in his hand. Behind his back. Which she doesn't.

She's looking up at him, like the pinched expression Werner has put on her face has carried over to him. But it's still a social gesture.

After all, they're only hitting her for dinner, I think. On her alimony.

They're not going to serve her up on a trencher with an apple in her mouth and the same hard, rosy china glaze I saw on a suckling once—*long pig*. Then why do I think of it?

Because Cutch is kind of looming over her, six-four to her five-eight. "Awful nice of you, Ma'am, when in your day boss lady like you would give water boy like me the white feather."

She snaps back, "What've you been reading, what'dy'a mean in my day, that was World War One!" But it's her last snap. "You mean you're . . . you're——?"

On the run? Evading? What will she say, if she can say it? *Dodger.* "Watch their eyes," Cutch is always telling us, "how they grow foxy with the law, their bones are loaded with it." Even Sherry is intent.

He says, "Ma'am, you think we albinos naturally like basements, à la moles, or something?"

Sherry says softly, "Moles are brown." It's only she knows his hang-up, like we all know each other's here. He's not even an albino, much less a black one. It's his put-on. He's probably only one of those pale blond types with broad noses and frizz hair; why he's from Princeton. And he's not evading because he has to, at least not at the beginning; he started out here on an exchange. If he went in for credit, he'd even be near the top; he does more work than any of us. Head to toe, hair to draft card, it's his put-on. Which is holding him up. Like a white plume. The reference, Dr. Werner, is to Cyrano.

Mrs. O. says nervous, "Oh, of course. It's just—Oomph's father is Navy; it's just her background."

Oomph says freezing, "Lean on the alimony, Mother. Not on him."

And I'm with her. Background—how dare *they* mention it. Oh I'm getting politically minded all right!

Cutch says, "Ma'am—I confuse all wars."

"Oh, so do I," she says. Brightly. "I agree."

"So do we," I say earnestly. "That's why he's in our basement."

Cutch flips me a look. Nix. Nix on the amity. And of

course he's right. "No Ma'am," he says, "you can't agree with me. I can't allow that."

"Daughter," she says, "who is this grand duke you've got here?"

Oomph ignores her. "Din-din, Cutchy. Stop being a walking wounded. Let's go."

But he's weaving over Mrs. O. and on his toes now, into his song and dance; how high he is will come out in the rhetoric. "You mentioned money, Ma'am," he says. "And I'll eat on it. Because I was born eating. But our agreement stops right there. So don't appropriate me. I was born eating free."

He was born like the rest of us. But he is carving out his doctrine with his bod. In our basement. Or the college's.

And Mrs. O. doesn't get it; he doesn't expect her to. He expects her not to.

Sherry says, "I'm feeling terribly depressed. Think I'll stay here and look around a bit." Her put-on is so near the surface it's almost her. But she knows that.

Oomph says, "Come on, nymph. There's always somebody at the Chinese restaurant."

What's her put-on?—to be ice cold, I think. And to tell us ours?

"Nymph!" Mrs. O. says through her nostrils and arching herself—maybe to remind us in the fifties she was one, once. And is still at her same weight. She flops in on herself for a mo, thinking, all hollow and tubercular. Then she says in her best high altitude maternity voice, "Where is this man Werner to be found?"

Nobody answers her.

A nymph is not the same as leading with your bod. Our night watches have discussed that. A nymph does it for herself and her *own* hang-ups. Which is why Sherry knows she is borderline.

Meanwhile Mrs. O. is taking us all in as if she never saw us before. In the way that makes you take in yourself. And not like it, if she has anything to do with it. Tell her she doesn't have anything to do with it though; she'll collapse. Why else is she hanging around? Counting for something with us is her put-on.

She says exhausted, "What is it you people really *dig?*"

We look at each other. It's kind of a pure moment for us. She has her uses.

Oomph looks at Cutch almost tenderly. "He wants to walk with the wounded."

Sherry makes his speech for him. Longer than she could ever do for herself. She even stands up for it. She looks like La Belle France somebody smeared a mustache on. "His granpappy fought to save the Western world for us. His pappy in World War Two just saved *his* world. We have news for you." She says it very softly. "We don't save. Not anything."

I say, "He'll eat you. But you won't agree with him."

He's our white plume.

Mrs. O. says, *"Oona,* are you coming to lunch?"

173

Cutch takes Oomph's hand at once; he knows she hates her true name—for describing her even before she gets to you. Her mission in life is to describe herself. Oomph takes Sherry's hand, to say sorry for calling her nymph. Sherry grabs mine, because she's so proud of herself for acting real. I take Cutchy's because it's the rhythm to, and because I deeply admire him for being so colorful.

And there we are—solidarity! E pluribus unum. We are describing ourselves. O happy, that's what I'm learning here. Put your put-ons together, and they'll hold you up.

Mrs. O. stomps out alone, saying, "I will not go to lunch with anybody holding an axe."

Well, you know the old; they're a value judgment for us.

So we go down to the cellar and have some wheat. The rest of the afternoon we spend making a huge sign for over the archway Cutch hacked out between our two rooms; it looks wonderful there. Black paint on the red top of the receptionist's desk we snitched during her lunch hour. WE DON'T SAVE. One of the Indiana girls wanders in. "What does it mean?" she says.

Anyone who has to ask will never know.

I am hoping I can live up to it. To all of my education.

"Cutchy," I say, "did your parents want you? Were you a wanted child?"

I already know about Sherry and Oomph. Their parents wanted them like crazy. And got them, Oomph always says with a grin.

"Queenie has a hang-up, she's always asking," she says now. She loves my background. And assumes I don't.

I let her. My motto is: Keep research dark.

"Cutchy, were you?" I say.

It's a temptation they can never resist, albino or not; it's sad.

"Sure they did, sure was," he says proudly. "I was the most wanted boy in Plainfield, New Jersey."

I am not surprised.

And it's all only fifty blocks from home.

Dr. Werner, maybe I'm writing this paper for *you!*

Maybe it'll help you with *your* put-ons. And you can tell the rest of the departments. Sociologically.

Oh, Dr. Werner, I have so much to thank you for. And so many new words to do it in.

Sociologically, college is simple, these days. And biologically. *It's the end of the secret life.* For any person who already had one to start with. Some kids, like those Indianans, arrive here without one, and will probably stay that way. But for the rest of us, the secret life—when it's out in the open—is very different.

Dr. Werner, you're one guy to appreciate that; it's right in your field. First day of class, when you define your subject, I feel that. When you say political science isn't a science, and it isn't even politics, I think okay, there's the put-on, now can he parlay? And when you never go on to say *what* it is, I sit right up. And say to myself, "Queenie, this guy shares your interest in the shiftiness of life. He may even be an expert on it." After our conference, I am sure of it. I rush back to the girls—I mean my roommates—and say, "Whoever said the faculty isn't teachable? He's very interested in things that aren't what they are!"

Sherry says, "Werner sure has the fault of being a looker." Gloomily.

Oomph says, "Come on, Queenie, freshmen don't have to settle for faculty. Leave that till we're seniors and shaky. Sherry, why didn't the kid tell us she was only holding back for somebody bright?"

What with the openness of life here, they can't help knowing I've been holding back. And with Cutchy always available. I can only hope they haven't caught on how far back.

So I daren't refuse the orgy routine. Not even if I had wanted to.

Way it happens, Sherry gets a telegram from her father, volunteering to pay for an apartment, if she and Cutchy want to shack up.

Oomph says, "Obviously, when he was our age they never thought of fucking without first thinking of a place for it. I call that rather sweet."

He didn't mention marriage though, I note. Wait till I tell my aunt, how the dirty bourgeoisie is closing in. When she and Oscar get back from Palm Beach. She didn't wear her diamonds down; they hocked them to get there.

I say, "Why'd your father pick on Cutchy?"

Sherry says, "He's the one he saw."

Oomph says, "Why a telegram?"

Sherry explains those can go on the expense account.

Cutch, who is on the floor practicing perfect repose, says, "Could the apartment?" If he could bring his wheat, he says, he would be willing to go. She could still pay for the milk. He knows a neighborhood where it's still a penny cheaper a quart.

"Pretty thrifty," I say. "Watch out for Plainfield."

Cutch says, "You sound just like *her*."

Both of them swivel. "Which?"

"We're all sounding alike," I say. "I've noticed that."

We all three turn on Cutchy. "What about you?"

Then we all three giggle. He has a plummy, furry voice which gets to a girl. To the two of them. I just pay for the wheat.

Cutch says, "Day that happens, I better move." He's testing us. He's not as secure as he acts. Who could be?

We reassure him we can't do without him, but he's still doubtful. "Her father's willing for me, there must be something wrong with me." Cutchy walks a very pure path.

Oomph says, "Don't you know the good old parents will do anything to establish us with a guy? Any *one* guy." Oomph reassures better than anybody. "That way, they count on saving us from the orgies."

Sherry says, "I can't convince Dad I *like* it one by one."

177

"Orgies——" I say carefully, "I've never been to one. All I know about them is from English thirty-six. De Sade. We have him for his relevance to modern thought." While good old Ffolliott speaks to the middle distance beyond us forty pair of panty hose lolling in front of him. "F-folly salivates. Very fuh-Frenchily."

"He dropped one eff when he was an instructor," Cutch says. "Put it back when he got his doctorate." He doesn't look at me; he is rubbing his axe with emery and oil. Oomph takes out her worry beads and nibbles on them. They're for men and hippies, and to swing not to suck, but she says any pacifier in a pinch. Sherry takes out her hand mirror and practices her tic, to show to her shrink. Nobody looks at me. At college, even among friends it's very daring to confess you don't do something. Particularly in this field.

I still find confession very comforting, Dr. Werner. Better than beads and tics, or even axes. Even though after nine weeks here I don't believe in God anymore, except when I go home. Everywhere else, He has let the world go hang. But the old habit still gets to me. As a monsignor once said to me, for me it is a perfect release of bad faith.

While what you don't confess to can remain on the Q.T. Especially among friends.

"Orgies," says Oomph, spitting her beads out at me. "I thought *you*."

Sherry takes her left foot out of its sneaker, rubs it on

the floor until the sole is black, and looks at it. This is her real tic, which she doesn't know. "Oomphie. I thought *you*."

Then we bust out laughing. And that's how we decide to go on one.

Cutch won't. Or not with us. For us, he disapproves hotly. As a retired orgiast.

Sherry says, "It's all very easy to disapprove of something for somebody else, after *you've* done it."

"I'm just telling you," he says, very upset; he has put down his axe. Very Eagle Scout of course, in the wedge it lives in; he wouldn't hurt a flea with it, not even an old one. "Dig, what if you three find out you even fuck alike?"

Oomph strikes her forehead, sensitively. "That word. That effing word."

I say, "We could try spelling it with two effs."

Sherry says maybe we can think of a synonym while we're *doing* it.

After which Cutch, as a protest, pays for his own milk four days running. He walks a very pure path.

It takes us that long, anyway, to find out where the compatible orgies are. Not that we're snobs—but on campus the computer-dating frame of mind is still very prevalent. It's not the VD we're afraid of, it's the personality quotient. Like finding the right coffeehouse for instance;

you don't pick your mind mates just anywhere. Or like on the barricades, you would want to protest with the right people.

The same goes for when you hunt for a group grope. You want to be in a rather selective frame of mind.

What you do, Dr. Werner, is get on the right mailing list. For hot news on fuck-ins. Frankly, the word "orgy" is out, even for your age group. . . . For the ones who keep themselves up, that is, which with your teeth and waist-line, you certainly are. Plus the way some of the seniors say you are hung. Why, you could fake down your age group ten years, they say—if you would consider not trimming your beard. . . .

Anyway, you're sure to find your level somewhere among all these newsletters circulating Manhattan. And even the boroughs! We even find one for Sherry's father's life style, which she right off mails to him. . . . I may even find one to include for you, by the time I finish this. Who knows, in another nine weeks of education, maybe I could fake my age group ten years up? . . .

Meanwhile, here are all these dope sheets whizzing across the island; Ivy League to underground, it's a new form of unity.

"And class destruction," Oomph says. "The City University registration can park its carcass right on the Park Avenue slopes."

I say, "And in groups. Which Doctor Werner tells us anything done that way tends to have more significance."

Sherry says, "And think how healthy! Because when you get right down to it, a fuck-in has nothing to do with dope."

Some do, of course. But a fuck-in can relate to anything.

For, in only four days of research—which is why I cut conference last week—we turn up tip sheets for every gender. Or like classified by intended profession even. Even for members of *Mensa,* that superior IQ society you would think cubical chess would be enough for, but it isn't. You can select from informal neighborhood arrangements down to very black-tie; there is even one hall that advertises itself *strictly* for exhibitionists. But basically, the basic human idea remains undefiled.

I'm a little depressed by one bulletin, set in antique type, which has already latched onto my two effs. But Cutch advises give up the struggle to be original while you're being educated; he's in touch with any number of boys living in college basements; any day one of them will latch onto his axe.

"You three plotting your pub crawl?" he says, and I admit it's all set. We are both mournful.

The night we go, he oozes up the stairs to watch us get ready; we are having trouble over what to wear. So would he, we tell him, if he were facing first a ballet grope—which we've picked as likely to be limber, then an art grope—because we are all three in the Appreciation course, and finally one from a leaflet called *Rabble,* which we hear gets the really exclusive activist trade.

"Skin's always in," Cutch says.

"Not on the subway," Oomph says. "Which is all we can afford on an itinerary like ours." And has our cozy furnace room made him forget it's still winter?

Sherry explains that since we are unknowns, we want to make a good showing. "Fur coats over nothing is too much like those call-girl jokes. Besides, we don't all have the coats."

I suggest, "Why not go as we are? With maybe a few mad touches."

So soon, there we are:

A leotard under a poncho—to which Oomph adds her mother's Indonesian silver evening bag in the shape of a cat—to carry our addresses in.

A body shirt under a ski sweater with matching high socks, which gives me the idea of the ski pole; we'll be in some rough neighborhoods.

Sherry has already washed her hair and let it out to sit on—which means nerves. And she is wearing blue jeans. Which means God knows what new insight. But at the last minute, she adds her old suede shorts.

When Cutch sees this, he volunteers as bodyguard.

"Don't be divisive," Oomph says. She wants to conceal from him tonight is just a tour. Unless we're taken by surprise, Oomph says, or enthusiasm, Sherry says—we're not yet really planning to connect.

And, Dr. Werner, do you know we have trouble! Touring, I mean. That first night's a fizzle; we might as well be selling encyclopedias. Half those bulletins must've been put-ons; the rest give the wrong address or the party has moved; we even go to Queens. Queens Boulevard, when it's snowing! Those doormen don't even know the number of the high-rise across the way, much less which of their own tenants is having a "community skin-in for all sociables." Which is the term the regional letter has advised.

"We've been had," our leader decides. "Or is this some jokester's idea of it?"

Sherry grumbles it is far easier to connect one by one. She only brightens when I remind her of the address on the tip she sent her father—in back of the bandstand in the ball park, on the other side of Old Lyme.

I do not have to be consoled.

And in the end, turns out we freshmen just take the printed word too seriously. Everything worthwhile here goes by word of mouth. Plus a corner of the gym bulletin board the Phys. Ed. people haven't caught onto. Bottom right.

For the faculty though, maybe I better describe what even a swinger like you might be up against. Because an orgy isn't just an orgy these days, Dr. Werner. Which is why I thought you would be interested.

Dr. Werner, orgies are not what they were. Or not like in English 36.

No masochism to speak of, absolutely no bullwhips— at least not in the college crowd.

183

And nothing in Latin anymore, which kind of disappoints Oomph who had six years of it.

But all those ploys can get along without it, believe me; as Sherry reminds her, you don't have to know the *name* of what you are doing.

Nature's what's in; we're young and we have a lot of it.

Unless you have a real hang-up; well these days, hang-ups are sacred anywhere.

But most of all—the trend in our orgies is to the affirmative.

If you could just take the message back, Dr. Werner. Oomph says it best:

We're not out to destroy everything destructively. We're out to fuck the world in a positive way.

Sound minds in sound bodies, and all together! Put your bod on the line for the universe.

Or at least for the improval of local government.

Ideally, every fuck-in is a creative thing.

But the night I want to describe to you in detail is the night I go into politics.

By this time, which is shortly, only Oomph and I try to make the route; Sherry has momentarily dropped out. She's always going off in a corner with just one guy anyway, leaving us open to "Who's your snooty friend?" Her alibi being, she makes more progress toward reality like that. And now she has got there, in a wild oat sort of way; her father is sending her to Puerto Rico for a short vacation with clinical confrontation—she's preg.

Which, even if you don't know who by, is a serious moment for your female friends.

"We go out Saturday night——" Oomph says "——I want it to be someplace with *meaning*."

And I feel the same.

We've already copped out quick from the Phys. Ed. secret program. Too many push-ups—and too many big, well-coordinated girls. A fast rebound to a French-conversation grope hasn't done much for us either. Endless prelims, which Oomph got impatient with, and I knew the French was terrible.

Besides, we're wise now that only freshmen go cruising. By at least sophomore year, you've got your crowd. After that, unless you're living with some spoilsport who doesn't approve of the open secret life—you find your goals.

"Let's be precocious," I say, "let's *do* that."

So, one fine morning, we shop the departments, and what do you know—if you look close enough, there's a goal on every bulletin board in the school. And since it happens to be the day after the President of this land goes on an anti-youth kick again, yours, Dr. Werner, is kind of full of them. We finally pick a tiny typed slip tacked to one corner, which says, "Declare your rights in rites, in liberal company, at a good Riverside Drive address." Top left.

Meantime, I'm suddenly in a dilemma I know by now is classical—how to tell your folks what you are doing at

school. My aunt and uncle phone to say they are back from
the beach. She didn't have her face lifted for it. But she
and Oscar learned to ride the three-wheeler bikes. And on
the bike next to theirs, they have met a tycoon who would
like to buy my big diamond-in-the-bank. He hasn't seen it
yet of course, but he's seen a picture of me, and considers
it unfortunate I am not confined to a bank.

I can see the three of them bowling down the tarmac, in
a huddle over how easy it is to lose your diamond in a
dormitory. I gather he might buy mine just to give it back
to me. . . . And what am I doing Saturday night?

Oh, family influence!

I say, "Date."

She says, "Who?"

I say, "Nobody special. With a crowd."

She says, "How are they dancing, these days?"

I say, "Nothing special. All together."

She says, "What are you wearing?"

I say, "Nothing much." Which should please her.

She's not prying, she's only hungry for details. And it's
not that I can't lie to her, by now. Only the more education I get, the tougher it is to know when I am doing it;
the difference between good and bad faith is different here.

She says wistfully, "I hope you're in with a good crowd."

I say, "Good? They're seniors."

Then there's a mutual silence. Into which she says,
"What is this party called, they don't do anything special
with nobody special and not wearing anything much? I

hope you're not *wasting* yourself."

I say quick that no, I'm applying myself. "It's a grieve-in."

She says, "A what?"

I repeat that.

She says, "For who?"

Here I have to think quick, since though from class discussion I suspect our goal may be general, I'm not sure yet. So I pick a certainty.

I say, "For the President."

She says, "But he's still *alive!*"

Even she is politically aware!

I say, "This one's the kind you can do it for early."

And only twelve weeks ago, I didn't even know I ought to know the name of my congressman. Or how far back he stands on what youth is for.

I still don't. But I know I ought to. And tonight I'll find out our whole platform.

So I tell her nix on the diamond; I'll keep it until I know my goals.

She says why don't I take the tycoon to the party anyway, he could maybe use some.

I say, "Uh-uh. Oomph says tonight we'll find out everything we're against. Nine out of ten, he'll be one of them."

What she says next—I know how far apart fifty blocks can be.

She says, "Who's Oomph?"

Queenie:

❦   THE GRIEVE-IN

You go *on* one of these affairs, Doctor. Not *to*. The idea being you are only rising a very little higher on the excitement circuit than where you normally are.

So that Saturday night, Oomph and I set off for Riverside Drive. On our way bumping into the two cookies, all kickied and curled; they are going on a date. With two scholarship boys from St. Olaf's who've cut the term short to come east from Minnesota early—which these two consider very dashing. "Enjoy your evening," they say sideeyed, and slide by.

"Oomph," I say. "They know we're political."

She says education helps everybody some. But that the most those two can look forward to is getting laid Lutheranly and separately in the back and front of a Volks.

Unless they are saving it, which I have found is still possible, but don't say.

Dr. Werner, is holding back publicly a revolutionary

act? Because by now quite a few of us silent minority—
who want world-selves but haven't yet made our minds
up on what to do with our personal ones—we're committing it. Like it's even easier than holding back privately.

What you do is play musical chairs. And get left out.

Not that I think you'd be interested.

But if you're me—the first thing you notice there is how
everybody's acting very nonchalant—like having four
hands come at you plus an unassorted head is simply your
daily bread. The other point is that when anybody does
get made, everybody has to know—it's only honorable. So
what with everybody seeing to it how nonchalant *they*
are, and *you* are, or emitting little savage cries to the general committee—how can anybody ever really say what
has happened with who?

But the most important thing is, whatever is not your
bag, everybody is very tolerant. You just indicate your
bag is something else. And if it's something new, you
might even gain admiration for it.

Say you're a girl, and you are surrounded by three or
four fat-bellies. You merely let it be known you're waiting
for a team of acrobat friends who are expected shortly;
you haven't been able to make it any other way for the
past month. If they're cynics and crack wise, let 'em; you've
already broken away to another group in a corner, who
likely *are* acrobats. To whom you can say in a moment or
two, "Oh, excuse me. I see my *friends.*" Just like a cock-
tail party. By the time either of these groups is checking

up on you, there you are having an apparent yen for a football type! To whom you shortly say sorry, but you seem to be building up to a thing for homos lately. Which is catching on from both sides, but is still fairly new.

All you ever have to do is pick carefully—and *keep claiming the wrong yen*. A yen is always respected by youth, Dr. Werner. Especially a sudden one. And so, hand over hand, tight corner to tighter, a girl can still spend a quiet unsuccessful evening almost anywhere.

It could even happen to a boy.

And, Doctor, it helps too that these events take place in a fog. Incense, joints or cigarettes, all according to neighborhood. Or political affiliation. If it's tea party though, watch out, the hop haze has to be gotten rid of at intervals, maybe air-conditioner if it's that kind of mid-dle-brow pad, or punkah fans if it's psychedelic style, or just a lot of White Owl cigars being passed.

Because the fuzz is always expected. And a party's made if they turn up. Doesn't have to be real ones. Sometimes only a mad rumor will scatter the pack. Or else a couple of very butch fags I meet once, masseurs on the side, who will hire out for the night.

Otherwise, it's very politically free, Dr. Werner. Just you on your own in the fog, with everybody else.

So I am not too surprised when that Riverside Drive address turns out to be on Central Park West. But lobby to lobby, grief travels fast, and soon we all pile out of cabs at the correct apartment house. From all those columns, it's one of the great ones, once. But now whatever can't be nailed down is gone, including some of the marble— and suddenly I recognize it. I can remember my five-year-old Mary Janes walking across sixty feet of Oriental rug. Nila's old place! Nosey was born in it. It's not a slum yet; there's still one of those foot-long Tenants' Committee notices telling you what to do if you are stabbed in the elevator. But still I lose my cool and say, "My God, I used to know people who lived here!"

We are crammed in that elevator by now, which is a slow one, and the griever kneeing me from behind says over my head, "You still do."

So I am covered with gaucherie.

Beside me Oomph says, "My friend here likes to hark back." She's not ratting; she has to constantly help me with my hang-ups.

Like I *know* the past is a property has been condemned.

She's from L.A. though; for her it's easier.

But still I blush my way up ten floors. The pack in the car don't have knives in me but I'd almost rather. Queenie, my one hot cheek tells the other, can't you remember? *Never hark back in a group.* In a group, you can only hark forward.

And when we get to that apartment door, on it are all the reasons why.

There must be thirty–forty people in the line ahead of

Oomph and me, waiting to study what's posted on it, and
to add their own comments. So I have more time than
usual to rally myself. Parking my poncho—they have
racks, this place is organized!—I see the usual leotards, but
a lot of the dress is more meaningful. I myself have a little
paste-on jewelry here and there and between my bikini,
but nothing that says anything.

Oomph and I think that putting a critique of our lousy
civilization on your tit is a critique on it. So she has nothing there.

But there is always at least one exhibitionist. The girl
ahead of us has nothing there either, but below, she is
wearing a cache-nombril, which I already know is a sort
of locket on a belt, to frame your navel in. Every time she
turns, it tweakles. Which engages the attention of some
committeemen. Wiretaps.

"Hell no," we hear her say, "I'm a chansoneer. This is
a mike." She says a PR man she knows asked her to meet
him here. He has kind of a crunch on her. "He says this
place is a showcase for repertore."

But all that blood and ink on the door up there, what
looks like photos of people in dirty positions—she don't
go for it.

"Oh, war dead. That's different. Listen, you must be
college kids."

Well, she wants us to know about herself. "I'm as broad-
minded as anybody. But I never vote, see? I never vote on
anything."

Dr. Werner, to say you never do anything, do you have to be a member of the proletariat?

Right next to me is Oomph, a girl who can't even recall losing her virginity. "It's like learning to swim," she says once. "In all that splashing, when was when?" She has taken to group culture just like to the water. And assumes my backwardness is intellectual. Which it is of course.

She's still attracted by my background. But she's not sympathizing anymore, she's analyzing. She says it gave me no room to rebel. One humble way never occurs to her. She takes a look at me now and says, "Trouble with you, you confuse these trips with being a professional."

"Coupling in *couples*," I say in a whisper. "I just can't get it off my mind."

She says, "Queenie, if you'll only just analogize."

I say, "I'm not as bright at it as you."

She says exhaustedly, "Who is?"

So considering all, I'm lucky she's the assuming type.

Because, though privately I'm still in a very romantic state—which as every girl knows means hot pants you know for what, you just don't know for who—I have made another rock-bottom discovery about myself.

I am not only frigid in grottoes; I am frigid in groups!

O boy, am I in intellectual trouble! In the halls of Venus, any *public* hall, and no matter how many corners it has—a man's hand on me turns straight into philosophy. And a woman's too, if you should ask me.

It all goes straight to my head.

193

Queenie

Dr. Werner, are you familiar with referred dental pain? Like when your upper tooth hurts, though it's the lower one has the cavity? My whole bod is like that. Just let more than one kind, loving person slide a little philosophy up my kneecap, and my brain kicks them off!

What do you *do*, if your virginity goes all the way to the top?

And in public?

By now, I can see through the crush that the door is really a huge piece of plywood, on which people are scrambling to tack petitions, or significant streamers, or to draw with paint and pen provided; there is a ladder to help. And a collection box beside it.

Which if you are me and stuck in the past, you think is maybe for the joints or the drinks, or to reimburse the owner of the apartment with a uniformed maid afterward. No eats, I already know; there never are. With some kinds of political action peanuts are ridiculous. And you have to keep your hands free.

But a big beard who Oomph is now talking to tells us the fund is for silk-screening the door to make like wallpaper. And a whole line of promotions they expect places like America House to be avid for. After which the door itself will be sent on a nationwide museum tour, under the title of our theme for this evening. We are to be a Collage for Grief.

Oomph looks at me meaningfully and says, "That's all right with us, we've been grieving for a friend all week."

194

I say, "Even with my astigmatism I can see that door is beautiful."

He says, "Oh but grief is groovier now, it isn't private anymore."

Oomph nods thoughtfully and looks down at herself and sighs, "If it ever was!". . .

If she had a hat and gloves on, instead of being à la Gauguin over harem pants, she'd be a ringer for my aunt's friends at the funeral parlor wake for Lalla, the first one who ever died on them.

And the beard—even in a purple singlet with the arms hacked off instead of a double-breasted, he reminds me of the dashing heir of the deceased . . .

They are baring their beautiful teeth at each other in the same grieving way—and so in decency I move back to let them go on ahead of me. They are ready for politics.

Besides, on my left, a beardless boy, with a pigtail though, seems to be indicating that he is ready for me. Also two on my right and one in front—is that a tribute! I am getting the prom rush, and I haven't even peeled yet.

So I link arms in the middle of them; it's always better to enter a party on somebody's arm, all the better if there are five of us. Even if two of them are polymorphous perverse.

So now, considering our goals, all I have to do is wipe off my smile.

Harder than you think, for somebody whose mouth corners turn up, even if it is only inherited. Plus my inscape. Which Dr. Ffolliott, after my paper for him, says is the most frivolous ever to come to his attention in his ten years of American Studies. Plus two years at the Sorbonne.

I tell him I don't mind; in only twelve weeks to find your inscape is kind of wonderful. "I knew I had it," I say, "I just didn't know what it was."

Meanwhile, me and my phalanx, we're the last of the queue.

And, in a minute and a half, I'm about to have the spiritual revelation of my life! Now that I'm at last in the proper surroundings for it.

And, Dr. Werner, *you* aren't there. That's always the teacher-student situation, isn't it? The faculty of the world! —against the undergraduates! After all our conferences, you don't get to see it because you're up ahead of me. You're already inside.

Oh Dr. Werner, that door!—it had all world-grief on it, didn't it? You probably passed it by without blinking; it's your department after all; you're used to it.

How can I extrapolate the parasociological effect on an inscape like mine?

Dr. Werner, we never had much world welfare in our family. The most was the donkey ads in the London *Times* my uncle subscribed to for other business— "Thousands of donkeys are being mistreated in Algiers!"—to which Gran always sent a check for Christmas. With "Albion" her terrier's name on it.

Plus my aunt's friends being particularly partial to those orphan ads that say, "Kim never knew who her father is."

My aunt and uncle read the papers, of course. And we had the human condition in church. But both the church and the *Daily News* put loving your neighbor strictly ahead of the public news—like knowing who's murdered in your street is what counts. Or else the palatial details of that tomato-sauce tycoon's divorce your spaghetti will be paying for . . .

Oh, we loved the moon walk! But like ours is still a village mentality to a citizen of the world like you, Dr. Werner. My uncle and aunt know the moon is our neighbor now. But they still go to Palm Beach.

"Not that they're dumb," I say to my roommates, when we first rap. "My uncle knows the world is changing, and is keeping it from my aunt. She's keeping it from him. And I'm keeping it from them. I come from very personal people, that's all. Some people are personal about everything."

Oomph says, "Three generations of women in my mother's family have been helping the world impersonally. And where has it got to?"

Sherry says, "Old Lyme is clean. But it knows very well the rest of the world is dirty."

Cutch says to them, "Catch that white racist complexion on the girl, ladies. Bet it's never suffered one international pain."

I say, "No, it hasn't. But meeting you three has been wonderful."

But a mass meeting is best. Even though all the others have gone ahead into action, and I am now alone with my two morphs.

One of them starts reading off from that door.

Oh, Doctor—I don't have to tell you! Grief maps, grief distribution curves—everything wrong with the world your whole course could think of is there!—plus a canful of bullets that have been in somebody, and a neat tube of blood marked "Not for TV."

Though maybe—did you catch that poem on a red typewriter ribbon that begins, "Down here in youth, our abattoir——"? Even in the voice of a morph that sounds very fine.

"Hoist me up," I say to the other morph. "I forgot my contacts."

With a joint tickle, they oblige me. They're two who don't care which gender they're with as long as they're together with it.

After a minute one pipes, "Let's go, dear. She's queer for art." The other answers, "But is Art queer for her?"

I don't care. For the first time in my life I am alone with all the grief that can be posted on a door and read from a ladder, and I am making the most of it! Of everything from which a happy childhood was deprived.

And when I finally turn around, Dr. Werner, I'm right up there with the rest of you. They could exhibit me in every museum of the country if they want to. My tears have collaged.

"Oh, why did nobody tell me?" I cry. "That the human condition is *current events*."

Because nobody's there, of course. They're all inside already, doing like you say to. Externalizing it.

It's only me has my time lag. Which this time, what it does is to keep me sitting on that ladder for quite a spell thinking how wonderful you are. Or were three weeks ago when you left us for your world lecture tour. Like when you speak of suffering *for* all the suffering. Like when you remind us all these causes will go right down the drain of history, unless we quick connect with them.

On that door is proper action for it. Petitions for every pulse, mass meetings as arranged!

But I am feeling more personal.

That's the way women feel when they get universally excited, Doctor.

God *is* for us, but there's a catch in it.

Because what I am thinking is—why just settle for an orgasm-in-the-round for the sake of humanity? Why not go all out and have a baby for it!

I find I am actually willing to do that, to declare myself at one with the world.

199

In fact, there seems no other way to say fuck the world and still put your bod on the line for it.

And personally, I'm thinking that if a man like you cared to put out a little philosophy for me—I'd let it stay.

Which is a good time to have a friend like Oomph.

Because just then, the pigtail slips out of the meeting and shouts up at me, "Your friend's in trouble."

I scramble down at once, and in there.

Boy, is she! As the sparks fly upward. She has tangled with the camera crew, which has been shooting a few promotional highlights. And has busted the lens of the mini that her pick-up, the crew chief, had stashed away for spontaneity's sake. In his beard.

"Who she think she is——" he's saying to his friends, who are dabbing the blood on his chin where she tore some of him off along with the tape. "A movie star?"

Oomph is standing there, harem legs planted, burning right back at him. "Peeper! Whyn't you put your whole life on film and coexist with it, then you wouldn't need to worry. You would always be there!"

I give her a warning look, same as she did for me in the elevator. I *like* film, Doctor. It works for you. While you wait. Which is finey with me. But on the question of film, Oomph's the oldie. She says it's the stockbroker in her coming out for active sports. Knowing her mother, Mrs. O., I'd say it's the bluestocking. Neither one of them can bear just to watch. Or to be watched. It's the one flaw in Oomph's modernity.

"My friend doesn't like deceit," I say. "Especially when it's done to *her*."

I'm different from her; I *know* when I'm ratting. That's my hang-up. But like any two girls going out for goals, it's time for us to part anyway. And I see she and the beard still have a thing going. Sure enough, a minute later, he leads her off to convince her about *cinema vérité*. The last I look, they are being it. Under a sign that says Fuck All Flags.

Because even though the room is as big as a ballroom, and probably was one, the arrangements are really ingenious. There's a booth for almost every gripe. And a sign above to show what you are grieving for. Plus if somebody would like to stage her protest on a borderline—like say between the Soul Brothers Yonder booth and the All Sabras Kibbutz Here—why she would have to be very limber, but her comment could be beautiful.

I also see that a non-joiner like me may be in trouble. The world is so full of dissent—and almost all of them are represented.

I may have a hard time not finding a goal. In fact I might get stuck with one.

Because, Dr. Werner—I can see a certain amount of arguing is going on, by the committeemen. Breaking away for your own personal yen is one thing—but in the field of world grievances it might be different.

For the moment, though, I can make like I'm going shopping down the bazaar. And, Doctor, a moment when everybody is being something you are *not* being, can be very educational. You see things. And I see—that underneath all the fine mass action there's some very peculiar flimflam being perpetrated here.

For instance, the very first booth, East Village for Mao, I see this couple standing there, like two mummies waking up to each other at midnight in a wing of the Metropolitan.

She's in her Indian headband, zodiac armband and Mexican bellyband.

He's in the same, except there's no fringe, just bells on his jockstrap.

As to action, they are like in a frieze—beautiful.

They are having a lipless dialogue—like the two of them have each swallowed one half of a ventriloquist.

She is saying through her teeth, "When you gonna make your move?"

He's saying through his teeth, "Now."

A long wait, then she says it again.

Then he does.

And if you listen close, you can hear he is making it. But at this rate it will take them two days to connect.

So I pass on to where a homophile for Africa is making a clear play for what looks very like an African for homophilia. Then on to where an anti-World Bankist is getting very cozy with one of the hostesses from Swissair For Socialism. Of course that's not too far apart ideologically. And he's only using his nose to balance a penny on her stomach, which when a girl is doing a backbend, isn't too difficult.

But I only have to pass a few more booths to realize what is really going on here.

World dissent is in peril here! People are agreeing with one another.

And mass action is in trouble too. Couples are trying to *connect*.

But don't worry, Dr. Werner. Wherever you were at the time, your steering committee is very alert.

What really tips them off is the chansoneer. Something has excited that girl.

She is on the speaker's dais, in the middle of the floor, in front of the atrocity blowups. She's putting her bod on the line all right. For herself! And the guy she's with of course. Who must be the public relations man. And boy—do they know show biz.

You have a marvelously handsome steering committee, Dr. Werner. The way the best politicals ought to be. They are in there on the double. At first, the way those studs of yours grab the girls and vice versa, some dopes might think those opportunists were just going into action for themselves. But in a minute, we can all see how selfless they are. Mass action is what they're after! Public brawls— with plenty of infighting! Those smart dogs are helping everybody put his bod on the line—together.

203

And in less than ten minutes—what do we have but a classic instance of revolutionary action!

Like you say in conference, even young people can see what time means, if they try! Because here was a ballroom where people of the old regime never did anything but maybe shimmy for themselves. And now here is a whole goddam hall of dedicated people, rocking, rocking together for social action. Collaging for Grief! And God, are they affirmative.

"Poison nerve gas!" a girl right next to me yells, rearing up from a pile of bodies like a Martha Graham soloist.

"Strontium in Utah!" yells a seconder, shivering out a leg with crotch evident. Then come "Tear gas against the marchers!" "Hormones in chickens!" "Thalidomide babies!"—in fact all the protests for the environment that you can think of—but with the gesture that is appropriate.

Gestures in favor of life, Dr. Werner. Postures for it. I have never seen so many remarkable ones. Everyone is moaning now, connections almost forgot. That's how selfless some people are.

But then your strong-arm boys start up again, with ritual limb-gnashing—and that takes care of it.

Some themes are more favored than others, and there are cynics here like anywhere; a guy who shouts he's doing it for the workers is hooted at, and "Vietnam!" doesn't make for easy symbolic humping. But like anywhere, there are also some lightweights; their great favorite seems to be BREAK THE DATING SYSTEM IN SCHENECTADY.

I horn in with them, since I am a lightweight here too. Because I am in trouble with my grief already, Doctor.

I have made the usual discovery; among yea-sayers I am always a nay-sayer. In my political self, I am a pig. Everything politics has to give, I want for myself.

Here are all these fine, open people giving their all for the welfare of all—and I can't manage it. My world-soul in that direction is personal. No matter how many people are in a bed—for me, talk kills bed.

I can have a kid for the world, maybe, but only in private. In public, I can't give myself for the world.

While to complete my shame, up on that dais, in an awed circle of what I see at once are the hard-core serious, I see a girl who's going all out for it.

It's the chansoneer! All she needed was a suggestive suggestion. She is going positively ape over the human condition. And these two morphs are being a great help.

I am just elbowing my way out of Schenectady, who are backsliding into couples again, when I hear behind me, "Not having it, honey? What's your bag?"

I say quick, "Oh, I'm a dilettante"—then I see it's the beard.

Naturally I say, "Where's Oomph?" To my surprise he fades, just like that.

The next approach is from a meek little guy who may even be playing my game. He looks awfully like a husband.

I say, "Can't stand the music." Which is electronic

Bach. "Want some raga. Go get me some raga. It's the best thing for labor pains."

He lights out like I'm asking for chop suey or something. I do like raga. For yen-over-yen, the truth is best.

And then I find myself at the booth where I started at. But what I am looking at is not déjà vu. Those two with the headbands, they have connected! Time was on their side after all, I was the pessimist. Though happy as I usually am, that's encouraging.

Anyway, those two—they're looking neither backward nor forward. And scarcely moving it. Like they are just saying—"Hark!"

. . . Doctor, when the world is swallowed up in dissent, what is to come upon a political action that is perfectible! There they are, working out their world-sorrow in the *present*. And I haven't even found my past yet.

Thinking that, I grab a curly-haired boy in jeans next to me, and we start kissing up a storm. Then we both bug off backward into the fleshpile. I'm embarrassed, and so is my kissee, each of us *recognizing* a natural instinct in the other. We're both girls.

"Sorry," she says. "I'm not wearing my contacts."

But both of us are gratified—a natural instinct isn't easy come by, these days. Or this evening. She hauls out a joint, lights up and two-fingers it to me; I draw for a while, then pass it back, saying "Peace!" And watch her go down the line to find somebody she can make it better with.

I feel lonely, unstoned and unfucked, even dreaming of the days of yore you tell us about, when just not being a Commie was enough to get you ostracized. But now, even to be anything anti-anti, you still have to do it with the bod; anything purely mental is insincere. And I agree, oh, I agree—but why can I only do it mentally?

This is what I'm thinking, meanwhile watching a group in the middle of which is a girl with her face half around somebody who certainly isn't a girl.

Only this communal stockpiling isn't for me either. I'm stuck with this sneaking perversion for a twosome. I have come face to face with my yen. I am an I. Who is an auk.

And then I notice that the girl on the other end of that boy is Oomph, and both of them are being forced. Only he's beyond protest; he's agreeing all right. Couple of guys behind him are watching, and cheering him on in the modern way—but the guy who's got Oomph by the neck and from behind, is for real.

Or as real as anything gets here.

Because three others behind *him* have their cameras trained. It's the crew, getting their revenge.

And I thank God for the stuff that's being taken in here, whether it's grass, or politics!

For with everybody by now as stoned or as grieving as they are, almost all you have to do is point a finger, and like phantoms they fall back.

Provided you also thumb their eyes, meanwhile kneeing

them in the groin—which when the girls back home teach me, they never dream they are setting me up for a BA.

I do both to the boy behind Oomph, and pull her out— she's willing.

The three behind him back off too, when they see how I'm serious. A guy with a good camera in front of him is almost as sensitive as a guy with balls.

Then I hustle her down the long hall, stepping over some gigs on the floor, who are making it bobsled-style, or making like they're making it. In politics, Dr. Werner, there's more yen-over-yen than most people would ever believe, isn't there?

We get to a bathroom easy enough; the flat is one of those rambling West Side ones has about four; the first one we try is in normal use, but the second one is vacant. This doesn't seem to be the old-fashioned kind of party where people interested in intercourse go off by themselves. Or so I suppose.

I hold Oomph's head while she's gagging—like Aurine used to do when I had the stomach ache. There's something simple-homey about it.

But in the distance here, is the nearby throng.

I hear cries of, "Come on, this train isn't being made up in Boston." Like in that old joke, if all the girls at the Harvard prom were laid end to end—well here they are. I grab a washcloth, and hand it under to Oomph. Who is finished now and just looking into the bowl.

A toilet bowl is very philosophical, isn't it? Like a little shrine you can find anywhere. Manufacturers ought to put little Buddhas there, anchored so they won't go down.

"Well, I did it," she says. "I hope Mamma will be pleased."

So that's her hang-up.

O, Aurine. If she were here! My heart leaps when I think of it; her rage for me and at me would be so terrible. I see her, an avenging Venus, advancing on us to plug what can happen between couples, at the head of a great swinging, satin cotillion of the girls. Your past is no good to *me*, I'd have to tell her. Still, at the very idea, I feel my mouth corners turn up.

I look down at myself. Bod, bod, you're always still there. Going on seventeen years of you. Are *you* sincere?

My body jewelry surely is. Compared to the hard stuff from Cartier's. It's from the dime store. But that is absolutely all I have done for politics.

"Oomph," I say.

She looks up at me. From her washcloth. "What?"

"We have experienced confusion," I say. "But I found out something."

"What?"

At once, I have to hedge. Like always. If I say: I'm a wallflower in the modern world, Oomph—she'll say: "Oh, everybody has his kick, just find a likely wall."

I say, "I find out—that I always find out the same thing."

"Uh," Oomph says. She's looking at me. Really looking. Which, after her experience, is kind. "Know your trouble? You haven't enough hang-ups, that's all." She looks ghastly. "But in all that snakepile, in case you didn't get laid—that makes two of us."

I am stunned! The corners of Oomph's mouth do not turn up. But I have always thought it was heredity!

I say, "Mean to say you're still a virgin too?"

At once I know my mistake. So okay. Okay, the past has no point to it. But this is my present.

Now she'll put it to me, though. Why you frigid little voyeur, I wouldna believed it, she'll say. No darling—she'll say. Virgin just for tonight.

I could record our whole monologue.

Instead, she shakes her head at me. How, I can't express. But I know it's for herself. Then her eyes open wide.

"Queenie! You're *talking*!" says Oomph.

. . . Beautiful Queenie who never really says boo, Cutch always says.

Beauty's like film, Cutch. It works for you. While you wait. While you *have* to wait . . .

"Oh, Oomph," I say. "Inside me, I never stop."

What she does then—she gives me the other end of that washcloth. And we stand there, holding it. Female kinship, Dr. Werner—it's not as fat-tongued as Damon and Pythias. *Can* all the man-talk, our little smiles are saying. We're just two girls holding onto the same rag.

So there we are, kind of clutching each other mentally, when the door opens and in walks the beard.

With a girl from school—one of the rich ones. She has long blonde hair almost to the top of her hundred-dollar boots, and nothing in between, except on a piece of grocer's string around her neck one of her father's 2000 B.C. five-thousand-dollar Luristan bronzes. And as you say, Dr. Werner—a conspicuous waste.

The two of them start to back out. But Oomph gives me a smart push, and bows them in. "Imagine you two'll need your privacy," she says, and closes the bathroom door on them.

I say, "What's with you and him?"

She says, "The crew started taking a pic of us again. And he lost it. Right in front of his friends."

I say, "That why they gang you?"

She says, "Oh, me yelling 'Screw the revolution!'—maybe they misinterpreted."

I say, "Wait 'til he finds out *she* can't make it unless there's a bidet."

We stand there deep in thought.

Oomph is really a brilliant administrator. She turns the lock on them.

Then we scram. At the hall door, Oomph strikes her forehead in that way she has. "Wait here, huh? Gotta go back."

She takes her time. I need to go, so I duck in the last

john I see down the hall. Which has the light on, and the door ajar.

Oh, Dr. Werner.

Spiritual revelation is enough for one evening. Without getting the facts, too . . .

I know it's you at once of course. Naked though you are, I'd know you anywhere. Even with your beard untrimmed, even with the beret. Even with the earring. Put two and two together, top and bottom, and still I get Werner. That must have been some lecture tour.

You're still with your age group though. Before you could do it, you had to find a place for it.

And you're still acting in good faith. What you and she are doing is rather conservative. But it isn't science. And it certainly isn't politics.

I know who *she* is of course. Even in the nude, five wedding bands can be very characteristic. Even with her head on your shoulder, that fifty-dollar streak job is no freshman's. And like always when she's comfortable, she's kicked off those alligator pumps.

She had to be where we are; that's her hang-up. But being an oldie, she went right to the top.

So that explains who slams the door on the two of you, Dr. Werner.

Because I hear Oomph coming back.

So with apologies, that explains why I lock it.

Serves you right, really. That was no place to bring a lady like Mrs. O.

212

Oh Dr. Werner. If you and I weren't so hot for vision, we could lead a practical life!

So then I rush Oomph out. But at the elevator, I tell her to hold the button. "Forgot something. Be right back."

In front of that door, it's peaceful now. Woe has come and gone. All that sincerity ought to make a wonderful wallpaper, though. I decide to add a woe of mine.

Which I do very small, choosing a black marking pen and signing my full name. Then I put a buck in the collection box. Then I stand there, listening.

Plenty of finks like me have left, but some of the faithful are still grieving. And somebody should give them a hand.

I take a long breath—a penthouse childhood lets you yodel freely; mine can be heard a block away—and I let go.

On the bus we luck into, which is parked while the driver files his nails, we look back. Yes, people are streaming out of there. When the bus starts up, takes us ten blocks to catch our breath.

I say to Oomph, "What did you go back for?"

She says, "My worry beads."

Ten blocks later, Oomph says to me, "I heard you yell. But not what."

I say—"The fuzz!"

When we get to the dorm, Sherry is back. Cutch has absconded to Canada, then turned around and given him-

213

self up to the inquisition in Plainfield. Which he's wired
her he can do with more honor, since the local draft board
there will be extra hard on him; his father is one of them.
His message to us is: It's now a question of whether his
or the war's put-on will hold out.

Sherry's hasn't. She's all cleaned up to go on over there.

Mine hasn't. "Personally," I say, "I'm terribly tired of
holding out."

Oomph's hasn't. She says, "Or if you're not sure anymore what to hold out for."

The atmosphere in the room is triple gloomy—we are
holding up the world together, but we are having trouble.
And we miss Cutch's axe.

Just then the door busts open, and in march the two
cookies. They have lost their corsages, but they are carrying banners.

"We wanted you to be the first to know," they sing out,
and march off again. The banners say: "Dropping Out!"

Not that we three haven't thought of it. But who would
want to be a minority along with those two?

So there we are, stuck with holding up the world for
them.

Suddenly Sherry flumps out of bed and goes over to
that old WE DON'T SAVE sign of ours, grabs out a big sheet
of paper and covers the first two words, so it now reads
SAVE. Oomph gets the idea, jumps up and shifts the paper
so it reads WE SAVE. We start playing tic-tac-toe, adding
all the variations we can think of, including SAVE US. In

the end, I get left with the DON'T. Nobody says a word when I turn the thing on its side.

At about five A.M. for us ceiling starers, I say, "We could pray."

They act like I'm cracking, but they grumble out of bed and down anyway, one to a bed.

Sherry says, "What do we pray for?"

I say, "The praying's the point of it."

Oomph says, "Now my knees have done everything."

After that, we are stuck. There's so much world welfare. Ours and other people's.

Inside me, of course, I'm still talking about mine.

Oomph dear, I'm saying, you'll always have to do it for a reason. You're an intellectual. But I think for me, do-ing it for civil rights, or for diamonds either, is out.

Aurine dear, I'm saying, I went to the party. I went to find out my kick. And I found it. Some of those bods I saw were fine. Or would be under other circumstances. But I promise you, I won't waste myself. I want a young man to be fucking me, not the world.

So that's my discovery, both of you.

Doing it for no reason must be best.

Now can we all stop saying *fuck?* Because it embarrasses me. Maybe when I have the big Anglo-Saxon moment it-self, I'll feel different.

But the two of them are still waiting for me to pray, I

see. I have to shut up inside for once, and start talking.

"Oh girls——" I say, "I know now what politics is. It's when you are the victim of *other* people's backgrounds."

Sherry says, "But how is that going to help Cutch?"

Oomph says, "And how is helping Cutch going to help us?"

Then we see the sun is coming up. Who knows, maybe we helped it. And we get back to bed.

From her bed Sherry says, very soft, "The climate of Puerto Rico is very mild."

From hers Oomph says, even softer, "Thank you for trying, Queenie. But I *saw* them."

In mine, I sit straight up. I'm *talking*. "Oh, happy, happy, happy!" I yell. "I'm not happy anymore."

HARK!

T H R E E

Queenie: **DEAD WRONG BUT ALIVE**
THE QUEENIE TAPE

Queenie:

❦ DEAD WRONG BUT ALIVE

Dead wrong of course, the next morning. Dead wrong
  now—oh
But tenderly
Heel and toe
And all night

"Dead dead wrong" sings my little banjo
And in no mood to be right!

All along, bo,
To join humanity, Joe,
All you have to do is be wrong—
That's the song, that's the jive—dwba, dwba—
Dead wrong but alive!

> (from the musical *Queenie—An Old-fashioned Girl
> of Today*—copyright Raphael & Rey)

THE MINUTE we write that last line, Giorgio says I must
get out of bed at once, and cable it home. He says if every-

body our age could just cable that, even from around the corner, their families would be satisfied. Truth is always best, he says. And they will be so glad to know that we too are stuck with it.

"Youth is our real crime," he yawns, leaning back. "And they are in constant agony, at no longer committing it."

So I get up and go downstairs, which in any island hotel in our part of the world is never far. Cabling home is a luxury I never tire of—how the truth must be piling up on Fifty-Seventh Street! English negligees make me feel lavish too. Italian sandals for the scorpions; a note for civilization—it's the leather they bite. Inner cables to myself are piling up everywhere.

And in the center is my little turned American head. Which thanks to one man's talent, plus an enormous number of what seem to be perfectly okay credit cards— someone is at last helping me turn.

So I write the cable as suggested. Adding only, "And in the Hotel Bienvenida."

Since there are dozens of those on this continent, the clerk advises more info under "Sender."

I add, "And in bed."

Giorgio says you dream what you get.

Because one morning back at the college, couple months after the grieve-in, I wake up and know I am right! From the beginning. A happy childhood can be tranquilized.

Personal despair is what counts. But a world-soul simply will not stick with it. And from what I suspect—in this connection unhappy childhoods are not far behind.

I can't ask the girls for sure, because morning is actually four o'clock though sunny, and they've already gone.

Oomph to Delaware, to one of her father's weddings.

Sherry to stay with Cutch's parents and meanwhile organizing committees for compassionate visiting, until she can get into prison herself.

It's Easter and everybody except the housemaids has gone. Christ has risen, and they are cleaning the dorm. With fumigants and vacuum pumps.

. . . I can hear Oomph last week, wondering if what she has found in her pants is one of the ichneumonidae. She was in my zoo class and assimilated very quickly. I can still hear Sherry scratch . . .

I am alone with my ghosts. And I wonder if we three will ever meet again in our lifetime. I have a premonition. Maybe it has all gone bust and I am educated? Too soon. And with nobody around worth a damn to tell it to.

But if I don't want to die a louse's death, I better hike on home.

So I shoulder my strap-bag, and start walking. Because the bag hasn't a cent in it.

Oomph borrows. I lend. Sherry takes.

Usually she leaves me a token. But I bear no umbrage. We're a commune—in a pinch they would do the same for me, again. With us, giving *is* taking.

And taking is giving. If you don't understand that about us, you don't understand anything.

I walk purposely slow. I'm going home in reverse. To seek my fortune there. And breaking in Oomph's fifty-dollar, bought-for-the-wedding shoes. She looked under the bed, but not under the covers, where I was wearing them.

In my bag is a critique on me from the Registrar.

Confidential, and not to me. But in the spring, when the establishment starts mumbling to itself, we all feel an obligation to ransack the files.

"Miss Raphael is a precocious young woman"—I'll say, straight A's, B's and C's without working!—"who has not yet adjusted to college life." Who they are talking to, we have never yet found out.

But Sherry's comment is a comfort to me. "In that position college is only an adjective. The noun is life."

So at about 110th Street, I drop a tear for her, into my own handkerchief. Which is wrapped around her new passport I already feel she gave me. She won't be needing it in prison. Besides, the name on it is fake. She looked everywhere for it except inside Oomph's shoes.

So, penniless and anonymous, I find myself at the north entrance of the park.

I'm the perfect candidate for suicide, but to my temperament that type of despair is not personal enough.

I'm also the perfect murderee. That isn't me, that's American parks.

So I decide to play Russian roulette with myself, and walk through. On a strictly fair bet with the cosmos, already checked out with the I Ching.

If attempt is made, I plan to offer up the diamond I happen to have concealed in a Tampax. Hoping to be quick enough on the draw so my attacker won't think it's a bomb.

Ordinarily, that kind of stash is safe enough in your bag. But I had a feeling last night those girls were desperate.

My bargain with myself is: If I'm murdered, I will never confess again. That's what the I Ching says too.

But if I come out safe on the park's south border, it will be a sign the stars think I should take my habit abroad.

Because what's really bugging me is that I've run out of interlocutors . . .

People to report to, imaginary or otherwise. Life enhancers! Father-images who can't talk back, even to the most original sin . . .

So from Ninety-Seventh Street, and way deep into the Ramble, I am very preoccupied.

First off, I am practicing my draw. Only in mime, of course. Each time adding a quick kneel-and-plea-for-mercy routine from my old acting class at Deforming.

Going along, I work up quite a little improvisation. Those are probably the most Phaedre-like gestures ever to be produced in a park.

Meanwhile, I'm progressing southward steadily. And though by now I'm deep in muggerland, and prospective

4

Queenie

knife artists and rapesters flit by, not a one draws near me.

Because all the time, up hill and down dale—I am also interviewing interlocutors. For the purpose of speaking boldly to the empty air in full Stanislavsky scope, the bird sanctuary is really beautiful.

. . . I try out Mao, Tito, the Shah of Iran, even a few female personalities in case a member of the Mayor's anti-discrimination committee is walking her wolfhounds—all of them on the principle that now I've been through the deity, the church and university, the only interlocutors left to me are in public life. But I get all the way to the Children's Zoo, which is still pretty safe even if you're unaccompanied by one, and not a single notable works out . . .

So what the hell, my draw is perfect by now. And it's one way to get through Central Park.

I end up kind of steamy at the zoo proper, and gazing at the largest chimp madonna, who is sitting with squeezed eyes and a smile, in a bowknot around her own child. Which has squeezed eyes and a smile. And is probably dreaming of being off somewhere, in its own bowknot.

Does it crave to explain itself to itself? How far down the line does spiritual experience stop?

. . . By the ache between my armpits, I'm about to have one. The best I can do is fold my arms around myself, in rough imitation of a lonely bowknot, and wait . . .

Oh, it's spring, I think shivering; maybe I am suffering from parthenogenesis! Human beings are not supposed to.

224

To reproduce themselves all by themselves, in whole or in part. But in my chest cavity where only a few weeks ago a thumping world-soul filled it, something much less practical is surely forming. Much more lost and intense. Like if a poem is coming on and your protoplasm is not fitted for it. It's nothing I could tell a zoo lab assistant. It's the sort of thing you tell a chimp.

Or ask.

O chimp—how was it for you, when you first knew you were going to be alone forever and ever with your lyrical self?

Is it a pink sensation, like swallowing your own tongue and slowly savoring it? Is it like weeping for your future in a dream because you haven't had it yet, and waking from the nightmare to find it's still with you?

The wonderful thing about chimps is that you can find one in any capital city. And they will always give you the same reply.

So now can I limp on home and settle down to looking for a lover?

Once you choose a career that should be easy, providing it allows for both.

Maybe that was always my conflict; now maybe I've solved it. As Sam Newber says, if you're a respectable candidate for suicide and murder both—what other road is open to you but art?

I can always choose which one later.

Queenie

It would be nice to have a poet in the family, but I'll never feel anything but prosy. Just put one foot after the other and limp home.

One big foot. Because Oomph's shoes hurt. . . .

When I get there, the air has that good deserted feeling. A note says Aurine and Oscar have gone to join the tycoon, in Palm Springs. His firm wants to buy the tenement block where L'Alouette is for an office tower, and rebuild the restaurant. "They'll call it *Les* Alouettes," Oscar's note says. "They think big."

Aurine is already doing it. She's left five hundred bucks in bills in case I want to fly down. Or fly "anywhere the world is suitable for Easter." And says please to look on the hall table for my mail.

I glide by without stopping. There's only a thick letter that must have my midterm grades on it. This time of year, there should have been a postcard.

On Gran's TV, I see the fifty bucks for the burglar has increased to sixty-five.

Inflation is everywhere, even in my aunt and uncle's relationship.

What are those two doing, traveling with a third anyway? Catch me somebody, before my education is complete.

Up, up quick to the attic, where a young girl can still be naïve. You get what you can dream. You dream what you can get.

I spend the night pawing through my trunkful of adolescent drawings, composition, jingles, part-songs—including a requiem for several animals, to see if I can turn up a career there.

Even finding some lines On My Narcissism, an early *pensée:*

> I know the cold raptures of my own skin
> Dark behind it is the room with no loves
> In the gilding light my naked figure, a Braque violin.

I've done everything too young—except for what counts.

The whole trouble with living is you don't start with a requisite knowledge of yourself. Ought to be given you at birth like a pedigree—or a horoscope in which you can believe. Like, "Fucking won't really interest you. For you marriage with an old man—you haven't enough energy for a career." That's not me, of course.

My trusty little tape recorder is there of course, in with all those cassettes. They're not art, they're me, but maybe some kind of a switch can be made. Hang your childhood on a limb, your mike around your neck, and start wandering.

Maybe family confession is best.

. . . Maybe if I sit quite still by the telly and tape nothing, somebody will come and burgle me. . . .

Tell me a movie, Gran. In the studio of my heart.

Yes love. It's called *She Dreams of Him.*

She dreams of him. A *Green Mansions* bird boy? A *Cheri?* No, this is America. And not a belle epoque.

227

Queenie

I suppose a man like any girl of today puts together, made of sneak dreaming and open viewing?

Or maybe some lost grocery boy of infancy, with homburg-ribbon father-image bound round him like black sticking tape?

Along with whatever NBC daytime can tell me about that lost platonic half of ourselves we want to go to bed with.

. . . Is it a twin she wants, you viewers? A not impossible American male who is not a virgin at heart?

Not a roué—they always have bad breath. And are not really intelligent.

Not an Oscar—he's a husband. Though a good uncle. Bad husbands, that's what the weak protectors are. And the good ones are tyrants, beating you with their money belts. They don't know about love—that's what they keep you for.

Go, go, Granny, what if it should be love she's dreaming of?

I look down at my tapes all neat in their bag. The Piranesi Tape. The Father Detwiler one. The Monsignor. The Werner one.

O Channel Two, let *me* tell *you* . . .

Then the bottom drops out of unreality.

Above the telly, one of the ikons is gone! One of the St. Georges—that old tycoon. So the two of them are paying their own way down there after all. Or could the ikon

have gone sometime back, toward a silly girl's education?
That hits me, like a *pensée*.

Doesn't seem to be anything left to do but look at my
grades.

Which now I have my contacts in, I see the postmark is
from Brazil, or the Argentine, or the Philippines. Somewhere on the Spanish Main. But I'm not one to stop to
smell a letter to see what disease it brings, before I open it.

Out falls his card. With that half-yearly scrawl you can
spend a year deciphering.

What makes the envelope thick is the poem. Which is
typed in the same red, but this time is signed. So I can
read it easy, and all over again. "Down here in youth, our
abattoir——"

So that louse has poems like this in his psyche. I'll bet
he can beat any guys he meets in the ring.

But it's the card that I cry over.

That door at the grieve-in has traveled so far. That
sincere door, with my name very small on it, and what I
wrote. Turning up for him to read, across all the waving
pampas, and the Roll-on-thou-deep-dark Byronic seas.

How was I to know what world concern could bring me
personally?

And that I too am a cause going down the drain of history? I can read it in my own words, copied right there on
the card. "Oh why don't people remember that they forget?"

Isn't that poignant?

Queenie

I can't cry with contacts in. Besides, if you're crying
for just everybody, it doesn't last long.
Also the return address on the envelope is illegible.
So I have to phone Palm Springs.

Aurine comes on suspiciously full of fancy nonchalance,
like the mother of the bride. But it's Oscar who reads me
that envelope. He always knows where those two are; he's
Tekla's executor. His voice comes over just the same—full
of aphorisms for me to quote later. "Old people are each
other's executors, Queenie. They have to keep in touch."

The tycoon is real enough, I hear, though he's no longer
down there. They've discovered what he really wants is
this house.

I've been spared one thing though that hit me the
minute I smelled setup—he's not Giorgio.

But the two of them can tell that romance is what I've
come down to. And that I intend to be practical about it.

"It's as hard a place to get to as Cuba," Oscar says. "You
have to be hijacked there too." But he has faith in me.
He tells me from where.

I say, "Aurine—I'm taking my diamond along."

She says, "Of course, dear. You may need it someday.
For Giorgio."

I almost start to cry again.

"Aurine," I whisper, "have you any suggestions for
carrying it? I've hit on one, but it's kind of *obvious*."

230

"Darling——" she crisps back, "but of course!" Asking them for recipes always energizes them. "Look in my lingerie drawer, to the left of the sachets. Next to my medals." Holy ones. "You'll find two bras Alba once brought me back from Paris; they should fit you now. Two gives you a change. Look carefully for the wee pockets—pity the diamond isn't *two* of them." How charming her laughter is when it's mercenary!—Oscar is laughing too. We are for his amusement again.

Oh it's good to come from people unconcerned with world welfare, with nerves built on love and wine without guilt, and money just a little tainted with joy!

"Get off the line a minute, Oscar," says Aurine.

She says there's a little silver-wire-and-mesh gadget I'm to take along too. In case I ever want to *show* the diamond to him. "It's called a *cache-nombril.*"

Oscar's still on the line, breathing omnisciently. "Life repeats itself," he always says, "but it takes a smart customer to catch the echoes."

And before your three minutes are up.

"Oh darlings——" I say. Education chokes me up. I want to tell them the truth, but lovingly. "You've been the best background ever. How could you help it's a fucking world outside!"

He's not going to be the first to speak. Standing there, taking off his helmet, why should he? In that white silk suit I mistook the back of for a pilot's uniform, his huge shoulders look as if they're shrugging; he'll never again be narrow enough for a tailor's dream. Oh I have such respect for him, he looks at least twenty-five! Burned black as his face is now, he still looks North American, and his nose isn't really broken, it's only more there. He has on one of those dark blue shirts men up home still declare their manual labor with, but I'll soon learn he'll just as soon wear any mild pink or howling purple that takes his eye at a stall; he'll tell me that a shirt can't express your idea of the world. Neither can an art collection, or a model factory, he says. Or even a small, choice guerrilla airforce where every man in it has cut his disc or two in rock.

He'll tell me they're only his ways of expressing himself. He'll say, "Queenie, the one sure way to express your view of the world—is to state your view of it." But just now, he's not going to be the first to speak.

And I'm not.

I can already tell this lagoon we've landed on will be so right for me, especially in an orange bathing suit. The wooden dock we're on has that dark green barnacle slime which can't be faked, wet and salt and full of integrity. And creaking slowly. Fish are down there, mauve and Matisse. The U.S. plane stands on the beach like a housefly on a travel folder. Oh the natural world is so full of natural metaphor—maybe I'll never need to talk again. Beachcombing the language nits out of my hair, oiling my skin with the silence here—maybe making just a few dolphin squeaks in bed. Night after night.

I don't know yet we'll be spending only one here. Restlessness is the real riches, when you're rich enough. Meanwhile, looking along the dock, I feel like a macaw in a monastery. Aren't there any women here? No prejudice. But when you dream, a nearby woman can help check on what you're getting.

On the plane, there was nobody but those same two melon faces, any-country color, with south-of-the-border smiles but no chitchat, even in the airpockets. I tried a rapport, saying, "I don't share the American contempt for tropical sugar republics," but they didn't answer.

They are now scuffing up the plane's metal with a sander, and painting out the number with a name. They're treating that plane like a girl. I have to smile when I think that, and when I see the name they're putting on her, in words I know from the subway notices: EL TREN. Don't leave *el tren* if it stops between the *stationes*. Inquire of the guard, or the *polizia*.

When I smile, Giorgio's face flies open.

When I laugh, he lets out the South American for ho-ho. Underneath, I can hear he hasn't forgotten his English.

We end up shaking with laughter at each other—maybe he can tell I haven't forgotten *anything*. But neither one of us is going to be the kind of crap artist that puts feeling into words. Or not the first.

I don't want any more interlocutors, not down here.

233

Right now, I'm out of the whole electronic, apostolic situation up there.

I've got my tapes in my bag, a whole dowry of them; if the need arises, I'll play them back for him. Now and then maybe, between squeaks. He doesn't look as if he needs diamonds.

But now I'm all talked-out and tentative. I just want to make my move.

I mean I want him to.

Later on, I'll know that's all he ever does, with women or the universe. Or bean and sugar cooperatives.

He says most men go from ideas to action; he goes the other way. If you can't think what to do, he says, act! Your muscles will teach you your philosophy. The brain is the biggest muscle of all. And the realpolitik of love is the simplest. It's just doing it.

Later, he'll say what stops him, there on the beach, is that I am still an idea. And not only his idea. This is what has him cocking his head at me now, those eyes of his every time wider, like a dog that doesn't know it's a movie star. And compressing his mustache like a man who does.

He's seeing I am my own idea. In fact I look like a whole bloody bunch of ideas, ready to go into action. He shrugs his shoulders, but I see he knows he's not going to get by on his reflexes. He's going to have to use his brain.

I just want him to show me how not to.

I have that quote On My Narcissism in my bag—but that's just to remind me.

234

I want him to help me make my move.
Circumstances are a great help in some situations.
EL TREN starts taxiing, the wrong way. Toward us.
How important wrong ways are!
He doesn't speak. I don't.
But making your move is different.

In bed, in bed, in bed.
Terribly warming, isn't it. Begun, middled, finished—
and never ending.
Doing something means you don't have to describe it.
But I'm talking.
"I knew I couldn't be honest much longer," I say. "I
always knew I'd settle for somebody real."

So here the two of us are, down in youth's abattoir—
but it's hopeful. Two happy childhoods are better than
one. And everyone knows this kind of abattoir doesn't last
long.
Nothing frivolous I have ever done has been so serious.
We are still making our moves daily, but have also
branched out.
Giorgio says, "You and I were born precocious just in
time."
Because the world is getting younger every minute, he
says. It's getting ready to be born again. "In the usual
clouds of fire."

Queenie

"And the usual pillars of salt," I say. The kind that shouldn't have looked back. "Giorgio, why are the pillars of salt always female?"

He says, "That's the kind of question only a female can answer. Or a pillar of salt."

When a man of action has ideas, there's punch in them.

"Tekla taught me a lot."

He's terribly proud of her. Tekla's in the ring herself now, in a ladies' wrestling program up in Portland, Maine. Her private life is resolved too. She is now the wife of a local minister, Unitarian, in his valuable colonial cottage—a nice mild guy with a flair for investing her stocks. All she needed was to be beat up occasionally in public. So her private-public life is now in perfect balance, though on a small scale.

"That's all people her age can afford," he says.

But for us it will have to be different. We have to be. Young people have to be the ones to show the world how to live the public-private life.

"Queenie," he'll say, "*we* have to act like the eternal verities have stopped."

Because, except for death, they have of course. And even it is taking new forms. The other eternal verities are all cooling off, he says. Like the world's crust.

I don't like to ask directly what the others are.

I say, "But older people say there's something bigger than us."

"Sure," he says. "Them."

236

"I wish you would speak all this in public," I say. "Then everybody would know." And acting it all out is so chancy. Like what we're doing now.

"Carita, that's shit!" he says. "Oh, excuse me."

In private he's getting very courtly, maybe he's getting ready to hit me in public. For the sake of the world. We are still finding our balance.

"Once you settle down to speaking, Queenie, your power is gone." Of course this part of his theory has great appeal for me. "In fact once you act sensible in any way— you're a goner. So let the old do it. For them it makes sense."

I'm beginning to know all the answers now. The revolutionary ones. And it's beautiful really. Sensible—though I'm not telling him.

And there are some lovely Anglo-Saxon moments in between.

And I don't have to say f—— anymore.

Otherwise, since his family's cut him off for a spell— they understand revolution when it has style, but his mother being in the ring with him sent a blush over the whole Argentine—we are having to be rather precocious about money. He won't come into his trust fund until he's twenty-one.

So where's it all coming from, the stuff we spend for all these midweek investments in little island republics, which are promptly turned over to the peasants, promptly turning them into Republicans? Or for all this jet-set in-

237

tellectuality on the weekends, when he says our business is to be where nobody would think. Where even *we* wouldn't. And never to think ahead. Or phone for reservations.

Although I am learning to be a very good, good front for him.

When we walk into a hotel on his continent, I say to the desk, "I understand in this country a woman doesn't have to be a man," and I begin to smile.

When I walk into a European one, I say, "I am one of those stinking, warmongering Americans," and I begin to cry.

But upstairs, if I begin to laugh *and* cry, all he says is: "We have a gold mine." A weekly one.

What kind of a mine is that?

And why do we spend the middle of the week doing good deeds, and the weekend sort of undoing them?

He only smiles, and says, "That's part of it."

When I charge him with being some kind of a dilettante, he says sure, a revolutionary one. "Wrong world, dead cause. But in the end, its unutterable fascination always returns."

He says I am wrong for him in the same way. In a way I am like world welfare.

He's a sweetie. Dead wrong, but alive.

But the worst of it is, when he does come into his trust fund, he's going to put it right back in trust again, until he's forty-five. "As a declaration of belief in the continuity of the universe."

"And of you," I say.

He says I'll never be a saint, but if we're still together by then, he may be, and he wouldn't want to be caught short.

"If I'm fool enough to want the stuff by then, I'll deserve it." Then he stares at me. "Why are you always sewing those f——g—excuse me—those attractive brassieres?"

"Because the two I brought with me are worn out."

"But we were in Paris yesterday."

"I know." I left an order for some with Alba's *lingère*. But will I ever get back to pick it up? We are in Paraguay for the morning. He says he is working on this week's gold mine. In other words, I think, our grubstake.

"Well, it's an attention-getting device. What say we go inside the outside?"

We specialize in places with verandahs. Copulating in a bedroom makes him nervous. "My father died in one. In the middle of things." The penicillin cause-of-decease being a gag put out by his father's wife, because she wasn't there.

Sometimes, I think I'm going down the drain of *his* history. But it's fun.

So later he's standing there, thumb hooked in his belt, nursing his navel. A characteristic gesture, especially afterward. Which I point out.

He says, "Oh I feel as if I've got one now; I'm earning it."

"Hmm?"

"Oh, not with you."

Hmm.

"Don't you feel we're all placed in the position of earning our right to be born?" he says. "We aren't born into the human race, when you come to think of it, we're only drafted for it."

Ideas like this are characteristic afterward too.

"I'm dazzled," I often say. "Someday I hope to believe it all. On alternate weekends. Or when we stop traveling. What date is this country anyhow?"

In spite of all he can do, I still have my time sense.

"I'll do the thinking," he'll say. "Your turn to act." So off we go again, for another Anglo-Saxon moment, which can also be referred to in Latin, ancient and modern, or even classical Greek. Anything printable. Down here, revolution and the bod are kept separate, at least in conversation. Political f——g is out.

I learn all this the first week. But nothing else.

"Giorgio," I say, one night, "just what is our gold mine?"

He's putting a bougainvillea, it looks like, in his buttonhole. Two nights ago it was edelweiss. "Why is it the U.S. always wants to know right away what a man does? We Latins, we might stab you one day for what we think you're doing. But we let you keep it to yourself."

"Then let me guess," I say. "Is it poetry?"

He stares at me. "Christ, no!—excuse me." Politeness to women and Jesus go hand in hand here. "Poetry is *public*, with us."

240

That's why I thought there might be income in it.
But who are "us"? I can't believe it's just us.

So I go along another day, thinking about it. Where
does all this money come from that we spend like water—
no, like aquavit, like Château-Neuf du Pape, like pulque,
like tequila. Sometimes even like Coca-Cola—always depending where we are. And why do we always have to get
rid of the grubstake by the end of the week?

Finally, I decide how to find out. I get him, one beautiful evening near Belgrade, after a long drive out over the
Danube, and the moon coming up like it had never been
profaned. Or been lucky enough to have a president's
name put on it.

. . . Giorgio's very bitter about that. He says, up to now,
living in a Latin American perspective like he has, it looked
to him like at home people our age wasted half their time
hating presidents. Father-images, like the papers say. But he
doesn't hate Tekla, who is the only father-image he's got.
"Besides, for politics, Tekla somehow isn't transferable."

But since the moon walk, he agrees something will have
to be done. He says, given the history of the world, he can
see some clunk claiming the moon for the masses. Or for
the nation. "But what kind of cosmological cretin goes
and puts his own *name* on it?"

"There was a campaign picture in his Fifth Avenue
apartment," I say dreamily. "Their taste in lamps is terrible . . ."

241

Queenie

The poor, wounded moon is meanwhile looking rueful, like it always has. Even in all this pure socialist air, it doesn't look any better pleased. Maybe it always knew what was going to happen to it.

What I am busy thinking—as I swallow the last of a five-course, Serbian-style meal consisting entirely of sausages—is that we've just spent almost the last of the money again. All week, we've been spending it like—slivovitz. Which though I don't usually drink, I find I adore. Giorgio says at home alcohol is a symbol of middle age, but abroad it is different.

So I lean dizzily within the crook of his arm, like the little asp I am and say "Giorgio—I know where."

Because I figure that must be why we always have to spend it all. He feels guilty. For spending *her* money on me. Oh—heredity!

"Where what?"

"Where the money comes from."

He does sit up. "Where?"

I take a deep breath. The only thing I haven't figured out is when he spends any time on her. "You're being kept."

Wow. He's like his father in one way. And the shiner he gives me lasts through three grubstakes.

I don't leave him. I have my heredity too, from Aurine. I already know I'll have terrible trouble keeping myself up to the mark.

But by breakfast time he's told me.

242

. . . He'd've had to anyway. You can't keep forever blind-folding a girl on takeoff and landing without her eventually wondering. Or keep complimenting her because she's limber enough to ride double-jointed in with the luggage on the way to the airport or the marina or the heliport, or even once in the very vehicle—I had my first ride in a helicopter and never knew until later that it wasn't a Pan-Am! . . .

"Okay," he says afterward, on the balcony of the restaurant. We had another balcony off our room of course. "Say I'm an impresario of the legit."

"Come ahn," I say, but tenderly. "We already know you're *my* father-image." We still speak the same language. When we're not f——g, that is. Which he's still very impressive at, for a man who's had so much experience. Spending money in any currency you can name.

What he's telling me now, I can scarcely take in. The landscape isn't fit for it. We should be in like one of those tropical republics. "Last week is when you should've been telling me. In among the sugar cane. Under a downpour of permanent-finish blue sky."

"Uh-uh," he says, "why the Danube is fine for it. Like that old show we saw once—*Beverley of Graustark?* A Saturday matinee with the girls."

He's a slave to his memories, just like me. But he acts on them!

He's a hijacker. Not only of planes. Of anything anywhere, even people. As long as the transfer has a social

243

connotation that is good. And the money we are living on is fake. Made on EL TREN, the island we go back to one week out of three. Because if you're anti-establishment, you can't have an establishment of your own.

He's an impresario of the *revolutionary* legit.

"You've got it!" he says, beaming at me.

I haven't, of course. "But who *is* the revolution?"

I can't believe it.

It *is* us.

Except for a few witty friends of his, talented lithographers, who help with the money. International colonists who can double as freight crews on occasion. Plus a few data specialists who spend their time dreaming up what are called Candidates for Transfer, and have never in their lives left the ground.

All of whom think of the revolution as *them*.

"Everybody has to be a revolutionary," says Giorgio. "On his own. The means have to *be* the end. And they can't be somebody else. Unless you're willing to kill other people for it. Which I'm not."

"Glad to know it," I say, pressing a lump of steak Tartare to my eye.

"Sorry," he says. "My genes."

There are drawbacks to a mutual background.

Just then, the waiter brings me a neat little piece of meat—Tartare is rather eggy—and tactfully goes offside while I'm applying it. For which Giorgio gives him a huge tip, in dinars.

That upsets me. "That money is us too," I say. "And it's
fake. And the Yugoslavs are so nice. That waiter—how can
you do that to him? Why, he's even a socialist!"

"Not fake, please Queenie. Imaginary," he says, sipping
his plum brandy, then mine. "Only a little more imagina-
tive than the dollar. And Queenie, please kind of pipe
down."

Because people are looking our way. The manners
in socialist countries are rather reserved. And I have on a
very democratic costume. Meaning there's not too fla-
grantly much of it.

When the waiter comes back with our change from our
bill, Giorgio waves him away with that too. "Can't take
dinars out of Yugo anyway," he says raising a brow at me.

It's true, I think. WE DON'T SAVE. But I never dreamed
how I was going to have to act on it.

The revolution is us. But is it me?

"Georgy-Porgy," I say carefully. "Explain more to me.
About our ethos."

"Christ!" he says, getting up so fast the table overturns.
"The way you women fuck around with thinking."

This time he doesn't apologize to either of us. "I don't
have an ethos, I am it."

That's my Giorgio. And people are looking at him. In
his white suit.

To pay for the table, he gives the manager some dollars
I didn't know he had.

"Well now, I think I'll go upstairs," I say. "And have a

few pensées. Revolutions are certainly full of them." It's not an invitation. I feel strange, immortal longings. I haven't put anything on tape since I've been with him.

"No time," he says. "We're flying out. Home."

"Home?" I say. He hasn't said the word yet. "Is it——?" It is. EL TREN.

"Gotta get back," he says. "Gotta think up another gold mine."

I take out my blindfold.

"Uh-uh," he says, "You're going to be a passenger." Seems we're traveling middle-class legit.

Because, since the world is still in transition—and we are—we can't always avoid the *other* legits.

"Gee, no blindfold?" I say, looking in the mirror. "This is one time I was looking forward to it."

But it's kind of nice, under the dark glasses I providentially had, waving good-bye to the manager—who since we didn't have airport fare, providentially drove us—and then entering the plane just like anybody, from the front.

And sitting right up with Giorgio, though thank God he's so flashy-looking nobody takes him for a husband. "Oh, good-bye beautiful Yugoslavia!" I say ecstatically through the window, on takeoff. "This time, I *saw* you!"

Though I don't yet get to know what we bring.

"Better you don't know," Giorgio says. "But it wasn't coals to Newcastle, I'll tell you that."

But on the long flight over he finally raps with me. Being a passenger is hard on him.

"Nobody goes for identity any more, see?" he is saying.
I agree. Sherry's fake passport turned out to be made
out to me.

"Nobody goes for boundaries any more, either," he says
squirming. Seats everywhere are too small for him.

I say, "Sit over on me." I say, yes, it's like countries
still having border problems. I can see we young people
have to stop having borders on our brain. "We must be
very careful not to have boundaries on them."

He says, yes, but the most important thing, your private
and public life have to be continuous.

"Oh, with some people they already are," I say, looking
where he's looking, at the couple across the aisle. We are
in a large plane. And they are not exactly across the aisle;
they are down in it.

But since a plane to me is like a bedroom is to him, we
continue ideologically.

"Queenie, the real world is really seamless," he says.
"All the seams are man-made."

"And all the money," I say. "So who cares, by which
man?"

He looks out the window, at that crack. "If you don't
give away your money, you're just a liberal," he says.

"Oh I agree," I say enthusiastically. "And if you don't
give away other people's. Until they get the idea themselves."

He's having trouble though, he says moodily. Sometimes, if a hijacked plane, or even a person, isn't just the

247

wanted model, there are as many objections as if the stuff came FOB Detroit.

"Gee, people," I say sympathetically.

"Trouble with a system like mine," he says, "you can't shoot 'em." His voice has real pain in it. "If I could only shoot 'em, everything would become clear."

So, he says, the only thing young people like us can do is to confuse contemporary civilization until it collapses.

I know the answer to that one. We had it under Dr. Werner.

And I am just about to give it, when the guy end of that couple in the aisle raises his head and says it for me. "Then we'll *know* what we *have*." And lies down again.

"Ignore that," Giorgio says in a cold voice. "Stay away from those ideas about starting the world up again," he says. For a revolution, they're poison. "Action is enough," he says, gripping his armrests. "Goddammit, I wish *I* were flying this plane."

"I don't wish I was part of *that* couple," I say.

He says a nice thing about action is, it doesn't have to be consistent.

"Oh I agree!" I say, snuggling. "It doesn't have to be consistent with the ideas it just doesn't have."

So we are just getting more cozy than revolutionary, when the stewardess comes asking for drink orders. "Sorry I can't buy us champagne," he says.

"Oh I can," I say. "I have a little French money, though it's real."

248

After a while I say. "Those dollars of yours—they looked awfully real to me too."

He says, "They were. What d'ye think we are, a gang of cheap counterfeiters?" He says imaginary money has to have a standard too. To back it up. "What you do with dollars——" he says, "——you get them *out*."

So that's what we brought to Belgrade.

I say, "But is that confusing *enough?*"

I'm no economist. But love scenes with money?—I was built on them.

"You know——?" he says after a while. "You're not as tough as you talk."

I snuggle deeper. "As you once *made* me talk."

. . . Always a lot of italics in these scenes. And there's a real Aristotle reality about a love scene in a plane. The time, the place, the loved one, all together. He can't get out. And you are not in the baggage compartment . . .

"Yes, I *formed* you," he's saying. His voice is holy.

I try to say mmmm-hmmm, but it sticks in my craw. So instead I kind of flutter deeper into his protection, twisting his lapels, poking his pockets as if maybe he's brought me a stock split, going all over him like the pretty kitten I am—but keeping it all above the waist.

Then I hear above my head, "You're not as coy as you act, either." I look up and there he's grinning that wicked bygone grin of his. So we're equal again.

"No, my superego always gets the better of it," I say sourlike. "Or yours does."

Just then, my fingers touched a round metal object in a pocket. I slide it out. Jesus, do I remember rooftops! "I didn't know you wore a Piaget watch."

He doesn't always. It's just that for hijacking, it's more accurate.

After a while he says, "Think it's funny a revolutionary wears a vest?"

Does the whole balance between us hang in the balance? Do I answer in good or bad faith?

I take a deep swallow. Those eyebrows bearing down on me are extremely beetly for only nineteen.

I say, "Yes."

He says, "Oh, thank God, Queenie, so do I."

He's misunderstood himself! He's in the wrong end of the revolutionary field.

Which he says can happen, these days, in the same way a lot of the bourgeoisie are going in for creativity when they ought to be in a bank.

"It's my muscles misled me. And that money. Giorgio Goodfellow—natch."

What he really wants to do is hang out in some dark-sweet, sad corner of the world, maybe even without any palm trees, wear what he chooses, regardless of the social implications *either way*—and write poetry. With muscle in it.

"Oh Giorgio," I say, looking at the empyrean—which

250

just now out the plane window is so stunning—and meanwhile all choked up with happiness because I know the
college word for sky. "Oh Giorgio—and now and then I
help you with a pensée! And forty years later—we win the
Nobel prize."

He clasps my hand in his, and we ride four hundred
miles or so in a minute of strong dedication.

Then he says, "Don't know whether they award that
thing to *couples*."

. . . You dream what you get. But who do you tell it to,
afterward?

Not the one you're getting it with. That's unnatural
. . .

"Well, I'm for quitting hijacking," he says. "But in a
burst of flame."

"Violence?" I whisper.

He says no. Something flameworthy. But in the field of
international repute.

I say what I love about revolutionaries is they are always
so international.

"Okay, you," he says. "Hear this."

It will happen during the next presidential election. He
will have to borrow all the money for it on his expecta-
tions, since Americans will not take counterfeit bribes. In
fact, we may have to use up all his prospects—which will
make us poor enough for poetry.

Because just at election time, he says, when even the old
roués turn puritan enough to go to the polls, when all the

babies have been kissed politically so they won't grow up to be revolutionaries—even on the very morning, maybe, when all is ideologically at a standstill in North America, and only the sound of the gumchewers is heard in the land——

. . . And which also happens to be one Giorgio Rey's twenty-first birthday . . .

We are going to coup d'etat the most important candidate of all—to *El Tren*.

I bow my head. When it gets to me. What is going to be my role.

O love, O life, O sky—no, it's dark now.

But I have a role.

My luck, it would be one of those daytime television ones: like "The guy has the ambition. Who's to humanize it? The girl."

Who if she is me though, is full of wild surmise. And even grateful. That she is not riding in back.

Because, O my interlocutor, I have found you! There you were, staring me in the face, all the time. There you are, staring us all in the face, from the newspapers to the telly, from the walls of our Capitol all the way up to a goddam plaque in the empyrean!

It's just my time lag I didn't think of you sooner.

But now I know what my tapes are for.

Oh—Mr. Pr——t!

The Automatic Pilot

So now, today is the day Giorgio is twenty-one. We're in business. And you, Mr. Pr——t, are like in the empyrean with us, riding high. Listening to my tapes.

Which have been suitably abridged and cleaned up a bit—Giorgio said, "Have a heart, Queenie, the man has daughters your age!"—and along with time out for a few Anglo-Saxon moments on our part, now give us a playing time of some five hours and thirty-five minutes, with a safety margin for any extra pensées at the end. Which along with some meditative circling in mid-ocean, or a little high altitude tumbling—we are informed your private plane is very versatile—is just about the time it would take us to get you to El Tren. . . . Though plans have changed a little.

Old-fashioned coups were only *action,* Giorgio says. It's *ideas* will prevail.

Takes some doing, either way.

When I first let Giorgio in on the tapes, he is numb-struck. I am meantime sitting there all preeny—butter wouldn't melt in my upturned mouth—waiting for him to sigh over all the lovely quirks of my hidden personality. Which is now being played back.

He says: "Queenie—we have a gold mine!"

I see myself: a personality cult. Briefly.

He sees tapes being sold at Sam Goody's, record contracts, television excerpts, audio-textbooks—"What department?" I say sharply—maybe even Carnegie Recital Hall with guest artists, he says.

"Queenie, you are going to help youth explain itself to the world!"

"Explain who?" I say.

He says, "Us."

Because it seems we are almost out of real money anyway. Second, he has always wanted to write a musical. He sees no reason why poets should have to write advertising jingles to cover expenses, or lecture at the Library of Congress, or be hijackers after the impulse has waned. And he wants to write like one of those modern ones, which are not so comic but plenty musical. He sees me as a cross between light operetta, "Dangerously near Victor Herbert in your early years, Queenie—or even Floradora," and broad *opéra buffe.*

"Buffet," I say. "The restaurant scene." But my narcissism is kindling to it.

I agree because he says the end of me is serious.

His idea is to produce out of Rio and come into New York billing ourselves as from over the border, from the half of the continent which is going to be important from now on. And we'll do it in waltz-rock. We may have to go to Paris, for a couple of violent, vivid rearguard arrangers he knows. "Because you are avant-garde enough in your sweet way, Queenie." And the combo will sell.

Then at last he grabs me for myself. And maybe him.

254

"Oh Queenie," he says. "Those tapes! Aren't we lucky you didn't go around just fucking people?"

"I had time for the ethos of it," I say. "And I have overtime now."

So for a while the abattoir side of my life is neglected. In favor of the libretto. Which I may be the last modern girl in the world to prefer.

I fly to Paris, bringing back two brilliant, blindfolded arrangers—and my bras. The two of them take to revising my memoirs with zest; when they don't, I do the work myself.

Giorgio finds an audience for our stuff on the double, through one of the revolutionary marketing services that maintain connections with art.

Which will buy all our output, if we keep to the middle of the road on melody.

So soon the island resounds with arias like, "In the Studio of My Heart"—didn't that reach Constitution Avenue?—and that cello quartet for two old girls, and two basso partisans, "Memories of Midtown."

. . . I am not too keen on the partisans. In real life, they never were there . . .

Meanwhile, I'm privately cutting a funky recitative called, "Female Confessing."

I am worried about my role. Personally *and* internationally.

"Giorgio," I say, "am I stretching my boundaries enough?" Are we?

He says we're doing what we please. "In the time that's left to us." He has a time sense too. But it's short.

Meanwhile he's whizzing around the world bringing back bits of countries to each other, and for the first time commercially. Our loan comes in, but of course not in dollars, so we are hit by the rate of exchange.

. . . The song money? That's going straight into production, Mr. P. To the Pentagon, for help with your part in it. Giorgio says, "One good young revolutionary apple, that's all it should take. In a barrel of young rotten ones."

Because that's where you come in, Mr. Pr——t.

You are to be his burst of flame . . .

Frankly Mr. P., I am even beginning to wonder whether I and my gold mine are not just a cover for the serious, mandrake side of that island.

Where one day, in among the upas trees which have been imported from Java to confuse the cover, I bump into a judo group of what I take to be hijackers extraordinaire, who are down there hardening themselves.

Already they are not flashy types. They have turnip heads, spade jaws and hair like the bad end of a carrot; when they lean into the shoreline vegetation, they are like gone.

Computer eyes of course. But anybody addressing a rally in a National Park area will never notice it.

And one day, they *are* gone, like sucked off by submarine. They must've leaned too far.

I say, "Wonder why the mature international spy scene doesn't get more onto us? Remote geographically, the way we are."

Giorgio says, "Uh-uh, we aren't their style of crazy. *You* aren't. Older people look for us to be crazy like them. In the style of the establishment."

So, except for one bad scene with the lithographers—who have made some perfectly beautiful G-notes that Giorgio has to turn them down on—things are all ready and on target. Who, up in Washington, is doing fine.

And except for me.

Giorgio, meanwhile is refusing the G-notes very tactfully.

Standing under a smashing orange sky, in an old Brooks pink shirt with the sleeves chopped, he says, "We are patriots. This is a patriotic mission to save our country. If you don't understand that, you don't understand anything."

They don't, of course. Because they have put *his* picture on the G-notes.

Then I stand up. I say, "I am not happy with the female representation here."

Oh there are some camp followers on the island by then, Mr. P. And even some wives, this being Latin America. What really's burning me is—I have just been and heard the ASCAP version of my tapes.

257

All the female part has been left out!

They feel it will not have enough impact on the international scene.

"But *I* am the reason you are all here!" I cry.

Giorgio says, "A typical female reply."

So it's the desk clerk scene all over. I'm a front.

But I am also a means who intends to be in at the end.

So I say, "Well, I'm worried about you know what. Our Automatic Pilot." That's our code name for *you*, Mr. P. "What you're going to do with him, once he gets here. What *are* you going to do with him?"

I see I have hit them square. Even Giorgio. Hijackers are like pregnant women, Mr. P. They have to deliver. That's all they know.

I say, "Instinct tells me he won't work out as a lithographer."

I see they agree. And could kill me for throwing it up to them.

I have brought up one of the central problems of life and revolution.

What do you do, if you won't shoot?

So Giorgio compromises on my plan. If I just call it instinct, equality doesn't bother him.

The cuts in my copy will stand. But pirated unexpurgated ones will be made available. And I get to make your tape myself, Mr. P., which maybe you are grateful for. Because it will give you that much more time up in the air.

Next day, I begin thinking about training for my role. Like shouldn't I be getting nature skills? Which these days means like get a pilot license. Like, learn the latest in chemistry, so as someday to be able to create food and dynamite for daily purposes. Plus a little remedial medicine to cure the ills that will come of them.

And maybe learn to parachute. So that if all fails, you can hop a freight home.

Then at last it's your day to be drafted, Mr. P.—which is a stale joke around the island—and we are standing on the highest escarpment, under all flags flying, which look astonishingly red against the tropical blue sky because they are all American. We are flying them illegally, but that's revolution for you. And that's Old Glory, around the world.

Our lagoon is lapping the landing strip, and some thousands of miles away, on a coastal Maine island, the friendly shortwave tells us, the little whitecaps are scintillating too. Island to island, that's the way we've done it. When I ask Giorgio why, he says maybe because mainlands have begun to frighten us.

You are campaigning in Massachusetts, Mr. P., not far from the stern and rockbound coast. Our forefathers may even be watching. Some trawlers of the usual suspicious kind certainly are. On our radar screens, every blip is where it should be. We have an organization.

259

Queenie

"And it's sailing weather around the world," Giorgio
says. "Also including forty thousand feet up."

The oldest lithographer, the establishment one but they
kicked him out of it, totters over and hands me a G-note. I
tuck it in my brassiere, which is getting pretty establishment too but I am stuck with it, and give a last embrace
to Giorgio. When we sink to terra firma again, it will not
be here.

Giorgio has heard this tape up to a point, this morning.
In a kind of convocation, they all have. Our rank and
file is kept informed—they're young enough. The whole
room of them. Around the world. Giorgio's comment on
your tape: "So far so good. Keep talking." And I am of
course.

And now we're ready. We're coming for you, Mr. P.
With your draft notice. You are our fantasy, Mr. P., and
we are acting on it. In an international hookup.

Giorgio's last words to me. On his birthday, Mr. P. "Hijacking the hijackers, Queenie. *That's* maturity!"

Oh, Mr. P! You are real.

So here we all are, Mr. Pr——t. Forty thousand feet up.
In a kind of bomber. At the last minute, plans were changed.
On tape, that's easy. You are five hours, and almost umpty
minutes—out. On automatic pilot in the empyrean, com-
monly known to the uneducated as the sky. In what por-
tion of it, will soon be for you to say. Because somewhere

during this recital, which we hope keeps you rapt, pilot and co-pilot will bail out.

But don't you worry, Mr. P. He and I have been practicing parachute drops every morning. Double parachute, especially designed for us, because I have never been able to make it alone.

By now, we are probably in what used to be the safest terrain of all—in the empyrean over America. And are pronto hijacking a hijacked plane out.

We couldn't leave you in yours, Mr. P. The private one. For the mission we intend for you, it hasn't enough range. What plane has, of course?

We couldn't keep you. Not if the whole country couldn't. That *was* fantasy.

When Giorgio hears my suggestion he says, "Cancel all snide remarks, men. They *are* deadlier than us."

Hear this. This is a tape.
Listen carefully, Mr. Pr——t. Somehow, somewhere,
I am sure you are.
You are in a new-type United States of America
warhead, the new model with that long, long cruising range. Longest ever.
The new paramutual, ultimate concoction one, for
which Congress reluctantly OK'd the bill. They walk
a very pure path of reluctance, but in the end they
always come through OK. Maybe you will too, Mr. P.

Queenie

As bombers go, this one is fairly simple to fly. As
bombers go.
Are you with us, Mr. P.? It takes a younger person to
imagine this kind of warhead into reality, but so far,
your muscles are holding up fine. When Giorgio
peeks in at you from the cockpit before leaving, we
are proud of you. For the first time.
When we turn on the music, dwba, dwba—we like to
turn on our own music—you are sitting there, with
your hands at your sides. Maybe they *are* trembling,
but we can't see that, the way you can't be expected
to see the ninety million pairs of hands who are now
your constituents. We're setting you free of that, Mr.
P. We're now giving you equal opportunity with all.
You are now free to eat if you can get it, work if you
can find it, talk if you can get someone to hear you
above the noise of the Automatic Pilot, to which you
in your turn are now captive audience. And you are
duly relieved of the burden of self-government.

Hear this.
You are now on a par with every citizen of your country, Mr. Pr——t. You are on Automatic Pilot. Your
hands are free and trembling at your sides.
And you have been chosen to fly a mission of the ut-
most importance to you and the freedom of your
country, Mr. P.

You are going to be allowed to take your inscape
abroad in the service of said country.
If you *can* fly.

Hear this.
This plane is fueled to capacity. Its range is known
to you.
The playing time of this tape is known to you.
The Fathers of our country are always adequately
briefed. Like the sons.
Sire—this plane is going at top speed.
A simple calculation will give you the time that re-
mains to you.
The tape will direct you to the directions.
Can you fly?

Hear this.
This is your direction to the directions.
Directions for finding keys to cockpit and controls,
now locked in accordance with Automatic Pilot regu-
lations, will be found in the lower lefthand pocket of
the co-pilot's jacket, which is hanging in the wash-
room.
. . . Unless it is hanging in the cockpit . . .
. . . Oh Hear This and all that, Mr. P.—but I'm
for the personal touch. This is Queenie again. The

voice of your tape. And mine. Like in church, we're
all members of each other, here. We're all each other's
tapes. Which is how the idea of drafting *you* comes to
me. In politics, people are the victims of each other's
backgrounds. That's my pensée, which Giorgio has
parlayed. We think it's your turn to be the victim of
ours.

Because I gotta go now. Giorgio's already crawled
out on the wing and is calling for me to follow him. I
can't jump without him. And he can't jump without
me.

Listen to him! . . . He says I ought to tell you
first, who you are to us. I say I made a solemn promise
never again to say motherfucker—besides, you know.
He says in this case, I have to get over it. Oh Mr. P.,
how awful if our first premarital argument should be
about you!

Listen to him! . . . He says you must not keep
telling people our age what we are. Because we already know. Why, everybody over ten in our country
is already an Alexander or an Alexandress sighing for
more of what they've already got, whether it's death,

disease, money or an all-time high. And shivering in
their beds because they're getting it.
He says, "Queenie, get on with it for God's sake,
just tell him we're a bunch of young hijackers." Because that's what we are, of course. Him—just a
sports promoter of himself, and host of an island refuge for tired young revolutionaries, where we can
all have a little gaslight fun. Me—just a nice semi-
erotical girl forced by the times to be demi-political
. . . And now he's even yelling at me. . . . He says
you are not the kind of role-player would understand *some* roles are real. "Queenie, just tell him
we're his sole link between the putrid past and the
putrid future. And now get out here and *jump*."
Guess I have to, Mr. Pr——t.
We're not ice-cold people. We're about as warm as
you are.
But we don't save. And we have come to the end of
your tape.
So herewith your draft notice. Which being the age
group you are, we kind of like copied in reverse from
Giorgio's father's World War Two one. He never
went, but he framed it.

TO: The President of the United States, Commander
in Chief of the Armed Forces: GREETINGS
You have been selected by your friends and neigh-

Queenie

bors, your public and private life now being simultaneous, your boundaries now being endless, to
defend your country from yourself, by continuing under your own Automatic Pilot until such time as you
reach a plaque in the heavens with your name on it,
proceeding meanwhile under strictest orders not to
look back at the country you leave behind you, under
peril of becoming the first male pillar of salt.

Now let us observe a national moment of silence and
prayer for you. You do it so often for us.
Because . . . I'm afraid my jacket *is* in the cockpit.
. . .
Fuck it mister, do like we do. Get an axe.

Song of the Double Parachute

Floating down, very fritillary—theory keeps us up, flesh
sends us down. This is the song of the double parachute.
Who wants to make it alone?
Rockabye. We're in the basket that brings all astronauts
home.
Far away at my ear, I hear Giorgio clinging to me. "Oh,
Queenie, there's going to be violence. He *couldn't* fly."
Far away in his ear, I sing, "*Hush,* we're the kingmakers
now. Coming down with a last attempt to explain. Rock-
abye."

266

What else *is* there to do with men who'll put their names on moons they didn't fly to? It's a matter of taste.

As we scud over pampas and promontory, Giorgio calls out: "Explaining *is* action."

Yes, it's too late for thinking. There's only action, now.

Giorgio says, "Queenie, you can open your eyes, we've jumped now. Wait'll you see the view!"

Coming down. Coming very softly down.

Thinking ahead is saving. I can't manage not to. So probably I'll never be a good revolutionary.

Giorgio says, "The only ones who can be let think ahead are the poets. They're saving for the rainy day at the end of the world. . . . So I'll do the thinking for both of us."

While I put one prosy foot after the other, and limp home?

In a double parachute, you can hear what everybody thinks.

I say, "I don't mind being a feminist on my own. Once you join the others, you're only a unionist."

"Coming into Rio," says Giorgio. "Over the silvery pampas and down."

I can describe Rio with all the ardor of a girl who hasn't yet been there. We'll have a silver pot for yerba making, a rug sold us for llama, which we'll never be sure isn't nylon —or maybe vice versa—and a year's supply of the pill. That ought to be enough for what may be a long, long weekend.

Because I'm going into this with my eyes open.

Queenie

I know I'm going to have one hell of a time, hanging onto the *pensées*.

If a girl comes up with too many, people say: "Why don't you girls just go around fucking people? Everybody understands that."

So do we.

Female Confessing. Recitative:

So, no more La Pasionaria for me? Tha-ats pop!
But secretly . . . after the first half-hour of so-
    cial justice, ain't it all shop? . . .
uh dress the *wound,* uh give the *blood,* uh lead
    the *blind* . . . and   then   Stop?

. . . Maybe after the first half-hour *everything*
    is pop—
andlovebetweenthelegs isonlypossible because it
    needn't take that long?
—Or between any places you choose, of course.
    . . . So here's my song:

(*seriously*) Ah tigerbaby of life, sucking your milk, seeking
    your vineshade, I know you! It's me!
Getting laid. And I just want to be. I just want
    to be.

(*naturally*) And who cares if I overslept?
I'm being *kept.*
(Copyright that later.)

268

"Rio!" he says.

Really, the best way is by parachute.

Come on down, Queenie. Cable me you're coming down.

Floating down, like I never could over the roofgardens at home, even with the biggest rose-voices booming in my ear. In revolution or in rose gardens, who makes it alone?

"Have a diamond," I say, just before opening my eyes. "Just happened to have it with me."

And we're down.

꿩 꿩 꿩 꿩 꿩 꿩 꿩

THE QUEENIE TAPE

IN BED. In bed. And in a Hotel Bienvenida. Who is this hi-jacker at my side?

He has a local newspaper. "Well, they got him," he says.

Somebody dreamed even harder than us. And acted on it.

I'm glad it wasn't us.

I'm sorry it wasn't us.

"How?"

"They took a poll."

I clop to the window in my mules, automatically watching out for scorpions.

The moon, though wounded, is still there.

And the revolution?

It seems to be happening to me.

Well, you get what you dream, I think. And you dream what you get. And I've got a new song.

I'm still talking, inside. But I'm not leaning on anybody. And not missing it.

I am on my own tape.

I go back to bed. But the bed leans against me.

It feels very nude here. If there is such a thing as a de-
gree of it.

I giggle, but he doesn't look up. He's my refuge, of
course, but he's reading.

I'll have to feel my own way, around myself. . . . No
innuendoes please, from the stands . . .

Then I have to goose myself. Because there aren't any
stands. Not on your own tape.

Well, I'm welcome here. Welcome, Queenie. Soyez le
bienvenu.

Been a long road, hasn't it. Clutch your knees to yourself and consider. How you finally got through.

I rub my eyes at him. "I'm awake."

"You say that every morning." But he smiles.

"Do I bore?"

Now that I'm on my own, the possibility occurs to me.

"Even under concussion, you have a certain charm."

Do I? Wait until he meets the real me. . . . So people
actually have them!

"Want me to tell you again how you got here?"

He's been doing that every morning for the past three
weeks. But I'm awake for good now. And I'll tell him.

"We had to get off the island, didn't we? They did.
Those two who were us."

He understands me perfectly. "Yop, the international situation got wise."

We got too international.

"But before we left, did you cut one beautiful disc for yourself, Queenie! For all of us. In a kind of raga rock."

. . . Oi hoi polloi, do I remember! *Hear this.* Island to island, with the whole world listening. Laughing. At the first coup d'etat on tape . . .

"Then the real fuzz comes, didn't they." Just as the tape is finishing. *Get an axe,* I say smartly. And up they come like turnips, over the shoreline.

Then I crawled once more into the baggage compartment, and got hijacked out. And into a bed.

"A bed is always *bienvenida.*"

"Hmmm?" He's taken out an old stub of a pencil and a pad whose cover I know well.

"Concussion's over." But I still know how to parachute.

I clip-clop over to him and take up the second pencil. The pad has two. "It's going to be *so* hard for her," I say, in a scenario voice over his shoulder and waving the pencil. "To hold onto reality."

I'm acting it out for for him. My autobiography. This is how we collaborate.

"Put down how, much as she loves him, she doesn't want to end up in his poem."

"How do you think he feels?" he says, busily writing. "When he finds himself in the middle of one of her tapes?"

. . . So I guess we're happily stuck with each other, in a realistic way . . .

Just then, Umberto the busboy—and the night and day clerk and the second cook—walks in as usual beaming, with the day's armful of cables. Actually his beam is slightly at half-mast because of certain head bandages, but we pretend not to notice.

I have never listened to so many cables in my life as I have since living with Giorgio.

"The Presidential Trip——" he says, looking up pleased from the pile of them. "Why, do you know—it is deemed to have had an influence!"

"Well, we knew it was *selling*," I say sadly.

Which up home when you want to do something flame-worthy but not violent, seems to be about the best you can hope for.

"Well, soon we can pay Umberto's bill," he says. Umberto owns the joint. "And get on home."

"Gee, but money depresses me," I say. "It always has such a direct influence."

And home this time means *home*.

He's opening the last cable. "I was sure right to sign that trust money over to Oscar," he says, pleased again. "Money just doesn't stick to him."

"Yeah," I say gloomily, "but it sticks to Aurine. What's she let him do with it?"

. . . Oh, I am being so gloomy—maybe my childhood is cured . . . !

273

"Oscar wants to back the show." He tosses me the cable. *Pleased and proud to help bring Queenie in. To any amount.*

We are rehearsing in Rio. Umberto is backing it.

"Not going to let him," says Giorgio. "Oscar'll have to learn to waste my money in his own way."

"Know how he was supporting Aurine lately?" I say. "Selling off his collection of antique studs." And suddenly I cheer up again. I can always depend on my background.

. . . Especially, can I depend on Aurine? That's kind of been worrying me, right in the middle of reality. And whenever I look at Giorgio.

Right now he's got on a scarlet T-shirt picked up from a voodoo artist in Haiti, over the last of his size shorts to be found in the Burlington Arcade. Both of them are muscle-bulged. All his angles are very intense. Since he's stopped flying, his eyes are wider. And his jaw positively protrudes with poetry. He looks like some overdrawn comic-book hero—who God at the last minute has corrected with intelligence. And every now and then, God help me—and may Aurine give a push also—I feel like marrying him . . .

And every now and then, he says—in particular when he catches Umberto gooning at me, but sometimes even only when I amuse with an innocent crack or two—he feels like asking me to. To elope. "We have as much right to rebel as other people our age," he says. "From the system

274

that made us what we are." And stay the hell away from verandahs, Queenie, with anybody except me.

It's a worrying situation. No telling how long we can laugh ourselves out of it. So yesterday we send a hurry call to Aurine.

Because if we do elope, how do we explain that to the older generation we're saddled with? "I could face Oscar," Giorgio says thoughtfully, "but I see you could never face Aurine. Unless you do it under duress maybe. What say I force you?" But I say no, she'd want a practical reason. "How about you do it to keep up my dignity, then?" he says. I say, "Uh-uh—one look at you and she'd see you have too bloody much." He looks at me squinty-eyed, as if he's flying again. "Call it the call of the wild," he says. "Toward the conventional."

Now he's down to the last cable, and though he doesn't mention it, there's still no answer to ours.

"How're we going to bring in the show?" I say idly. "If we don't let Oscar." And how're we going to get home?

"What *about* those royalties?" he says, not looking up.

From the Presidential Tape?

Up to now, we plan to hold them for charity. Meaning revolution around the world. Since we haven't got either of them yet, that seemed only fair.

"Gee," I say, "I don't mind if my art has to support my life." Like maybe plane fare to New York. "But I don't think it ought to support my *autobiography*." Or not on *Broadway*.

Trouble is, he doesn't think my tapes are art. He knows they're me.

And the one that is me now, is looking at him.

He's now crouched over the pad like a prizefighter, with all his moxie at the point of the pen. There's a connect between money and poetry, he says, but he hasn't made it yet. The thing about poetry is that at first it's very pure.

"How can you write it before breakfast?" I say.

"This isn't the masterpiece," he says, grinning. "This is the one before. . . . Where *is* that coffee?"

We stare at one another. Umberto can't do everything at once. But I have also been very obedient about verandahs. And yesterday, I pushed him off one.

. . . There's an end to everything, Sam Newber used to say. And credit, Queenie, is among the first to go . . .

"Got an idea," I say, brightly quavering. "Gotta new song for you. How about I act it out?" And getting up out of that bed, I wave myself slowly backward and offstage.

Peering from the dressing room, I see he is still full of dignity. I am meanwhile both dressing and undressing. I feel as punchy as if I'd been in the ring with him. So here it comes, Queenie. You are not going to keep yourself up to the mark.

When I walk out again, I am wearing the *cache-nombril.*

I have a good navel cavity.

So I just stand there. No hoochee-koochee needed. In certain circumstances, a *cache-nombril* can be sufficient to itself. When you simply have to show what you've got.

276

Ordinarily, he'd of hauled off and grabbed me. But diamonds make a man polite.

"It's real," I say, quaking radiantly. "And it's yours."

"Where'd you get it?"

I consider. "From my childhood."

"Where you been keeping it?"

I don't answer. Because those bras long since wore out. Oh, the cavities that women have!

He stands there, grimly considering.

Then he breaks down and says what he always does, no matter what I have on.

"Take it off."

We are almost decent again, when Umberto knocks. Since he never did that before, he must have been listening. He couldn't have been watching, because when he sees the two of us, he almost drops the tray. Between the bandages, his beam stretches to full sun again. Then he shakes his head and goes out.

The tray has coffee on it. And a cable.

I grab for it.

"Uh-uh," Giorgio says. "Let's have coffee first."

We do that.

When I grab again, he says, "First—where's that song?"

So I think I understand, of course. Our lives are in the balance again. He has to keep himself up to the mark.

"Okay, here goes," I say. *"Female confessing:* Recitative—"

Queenie

It's only the dream-half of it anyway. In dreams, you always hold a few *pensées* back.

When I finish, he says "Well, well. Up from under. In waltz-rock. But that's you, Queenie."

"Yeah, it's me," I say. "In good and bad faith."

He gives me a long look. "Exactly what crossed my mind."

And do you know, what with fooling around, we almost forget that cable?

. . . *(Who* am I thinking to?) . . .

When we remember, I say generously, "You open it."

He says "No, you."

But when I start to, he says "Wait. Queenie . . . our cable. I changed it."

"How?"

This I would never have believed.

He's addressed it to Dear Father and Mother.

Inside, of course.

When I can get my breath, I say furiously, "As if I cared who they are, fink."

When I can get it again, I say, "You over-interpret me."

He says, "I wanted to find out for myself."

He turns pink when he tells me why.

I've under-interpreted him.

He hasn't seen her for years of course. But he'd rather think of her as my mother. "You mean Aurine."

278

After some thought, I giggle, "Think of Oscar as my father," I say. "That'll be enough."

We tear open the envelope together.

I knew I could depend on them.

It's signed "Us."

After that, the answer itself is scarcely in the running. As Giorgio says later—when we're collaborating again, "Queenie has her questions. But have you noticed how the one she isn't sure of the answer to, she seldom asks?"

What I did ask is simple enough. *"Advise whether best for by-blows to legalize them. Have less than nine months to decide."*

And had to pay for by-blow as two words.

Their answer is simpler. "Take a look at yourselves. STOP. Then decide."

When we do that, we roll right over. This time only from laughs.

Because Giorgio is now wearing the cache-nombril. For safety's sake, he says.

I am now wearing the T-shirt. For Umberto's sake.

Navel to navel, there's certainly more behind mine.

But Giorgio's has a fifty-thousand-dollar diamond out front.

We are equal at last.

When we stop laughing, I say "Plus which, we're both amusing each *other*."

What could be more equal than that?

Queenie

We send a return cable saying no to Oscar's offer, thanks for the rest. Collect. But signing it "Us."

So by the time Umberto has brought us up a surprise champagne supper and gone off again—he admits he opens all the cables beforehand and says he was only being sympathetic on the verandah—the moon is once more coming up.

. . . Surprise again, all that champagne and excitement has shook me loose. I'm not as pregnant as I thought I was.

But that moon will come up anywhere . . .

From our usual dateline, in bed in the Hotel Bienvenida, we are looking at it. And I am remembering politics.

"That moon is about as political as I am," I say. "It's possible that if you could get to the heart of it—not just walkie-talkie around on it—you would find a moon tape."

Giorgio walks me to the window to watch. I can see by his face that it still cuts him deep.

"Well," he says, "we'll soon be bringing the show into New York."

He says Umberto has already good as sold the diamond for us. To a tycoon who is fleeing the revolution and wants his assets portable. To Palm Beach.

"And you've finished 'The Abattoir,' " I say.

"How did you know?"

"You're wearing your vest."

. . . And I'm bringing in Queenie, but privately. Everybody has to be his own revolution. That's mine . . .

"There's no doubt about it," I say. "Our private and public lives will be synonymous."

. . . And am I liberated? Or was I born free? . . .

That's a question I'm not yet asking.

"Queenie," Giorgio calls, "come out on the balcony."

Out there he grabs me. Just for grabs. "God*dam* the empyrean," he says, looking at it. "I still want to fly."

I say, "Maybe there's a way to do everything."

We are both full of the revolutionary spirit.

"We'll do it yet," he says. "We'll explain youth to the world!"

The view from Rio is some view.

"Oh, I will, I *will*," I say in my new musical-comedy voice. *Off*-Broadway, though. "And except for this once, I'll never even mention the word 'sex'."

Then we just stand there. For a moment in a language I cannot name. Holding fast to each other, it feels like the future might even be around somewhere. But I don't mention it. I'm not a bomb-virgin anymore.

We don't mention it. This is the secret life.

"The empyrean," I say hoarsely. "At this time of night, is still slays me." Blowing cool, dark and forever, through *my* spit curls. While all the grief is still wallpapering the world.

"Oh you cosmos, you're no cakewalk," Giorgio says, looking up, and holding me tighter.

Queenie

Well, I'm me, I think. And for me, that's something.
"Ciao, cosmos!" I say. "We three are all together now.
*Every*body's here." Over there, like in a corner of it, is
even my childhood, that big baby-doll.

. . . Ciao—that kind of hail-and-farewell word you pick
up when you are traveling . . .

Ciao, everybody. Hi. Be welcome. What else can you
say when you are traveling?

"Ciao, childhood!" I say. "Be happy."
I don't know yet whether I mean hello or goodbye.